DOUGLAS FORD

Who Dies First

VISSARIA COUNTY
DISPATCHES

For Jerlin,
thank you for the journeys

"Happy families are all alike; every unhappy family is unhappy in its own way."

—LEO TOLSTOY

1

"But You'll Remember the Directions?"

Steve and Nancy planned their trip carefully and took no detours until the very end. Normally, they would have flown to Steve's convention, but with airfare skyrocketing, they turned it into a long, leisurely road adventure, passing through towns and landmarks that took them to places they'd never seen. So before the convention in Pittsburgh, they went as far north as the Finger Lakes, where they stopped in wineries and got stupid drunk; from there, they went on to Gettysburg, where they stood before memorials and pretended to get stupid sad. Along the way, they argued playfully about which one of them should die first. Eventually, after the argument turned into a stalemate because neither one of them would want to go on living without the other, Steve casually mentioned his aunt and uncle, both now at an advanced age but living on a fancy resort island off the coast somewhere in the south. It was Nancy who said that maybe they could stop and see them on the way home.

"Maybe we can see the beach," Nancy said.

Steve didn't answer right away. When Nancy brought it up

again, he told her about his cousin Stacey.

"I don't remember you ever mentioning her," Nancy said. She kept two hands gripped on the wheel and her eyes on the road. Nancy liked to drive and did it well.

"Him," Steve said. "My cousin Stacey is a boy. A man, I mean. It's hard to think of him as anything but a kid."

Stacey, he said, had never lived on his own, preferring a comfortable, uncomplicated life by living with his parents. "They don't seem to mind letting their forty-some-year-old son live at home," he said.

"Is he special needs?" asked Nancy without looking away from the road.

Only the sound of the road broke the silence as Steve rubbed his chin and considered his answer. "I don't know," he finally said. "I don't think so. He works and everything, mostly gas station, convenience stores, landscaping—kind of an odd-jobs sort of guy."

"You should call them. Find out if they want a visit."

Steve held his phone, but he didn't dial, his mind venturing some other place. Nancy took her eyes off the road long enough to observe his distraction. She drove the speed limit, staying always in the right lane, except on rare occasions when she passed someone. Sometimes Steve criticized her for her persistent preoccupation with safety.

"Do they know you're married again?" she asked.

"Yes," he said.

"Then call them."

Steve dialed and waited for a response. The phone rang and rang until he finally received the voice of an answering machine. Watching Nancy, he left a message that flatly conveyed their desire to visit them, perhaps even take them out to dinner.

Then he ended the call. "There. Done. They probably won't call back."

"I'd like to see the beach," said Nancy. "I hope they do."

"They won't. I'm positive."

Minutes later, a call came through. Steve looked at the number before he finally answered.

"Steven!" The voice belonged to Stacey. "It's so good to hear from you. I'm sorry I couldn't answer. I came as fast as I could."

Stacey sounded winded, as if he'd just finished running a marathon. "Were you outside working?" asked Steve.

"Yes. Yes! I was moving things. Boxes." He went on to say he very much wanted Steve to visit.

Steve looked at Nancy with an expression of exaggerated pain. "It's not just me. I'm married again." He told him about Nancy.

"Do you have kids together?" asked Stacey.

Nancy heard the question and glanced toward Steve with an arched eyebrow. "No. No kids," Steve said. "Thank god." He punctuated the remark with forced laughter.

Stacey answered with laughter of his own, though his sounded genuine. "I would love kids," said Stacey. "Hey, I have a joke for you. What can kids make that no one can see?"

Steve held the phone away from his ear and mouthed *oh god* to Nancy before answering. "I don't know."

"Noise!" said Stacey. "But guess what. I'm only kidding. Get it? *Kid*-ding."

Looking at Nancy with a pained expression, Steve pretended to laugh.

"What's the address, Stacey?" said Steve.

"I better tell you how to get here."

"But we have GPS."

"Oh, no," Stacey said, "don't use that. It's always wrong. Never trust it. People always wind up lost trying to get here, and I never see them. Follow this route and do it precisely." Next came a flurry of directions that made Steve squeeze his eyes shut. Nancy drove a steady sixty-five, her eyes on the road.

After listening to Stacey repeat the instructions several times, Steve said, "Can you just give me the address?"

"But I just explained how to get here. Didn't you hear the directions?"

"I'm worried I won't remember them."

"You didn't write them down?"

With her left hand still on the wheel and their speed unwavering, Nancy held out her hand. Steve recognized a command when he saw one. He handed over the phone.

"Hi, Stacey, this is Nancy."

"Nancy! Are you really Steven's wife?"

"Yes, I am. Guilty as charged."

"Well, that's just great. I'm looking forward to meeting you very much."

Nancy smiled as a truck cut them off, remaining as even-tempered as ever while adjusting their speed. "I am too. Can you please tell me the address?"

"I just told Steven."

"But I'm driving."

"A woman driver! That reminds me. I need to ask you something. Do you ever drive with the hazard lights on?"

"Sometimes. Maybe when it's raining?"

"Well," said Stacey, "then at least you're honest. Do you get it?"

Nancy made a face at Steve, and Steve shrugged, as if to tell her not to hold him responsible. She rolled her eyes. "I suppose

I get it."

"I spend a lot of time making up jokes," said Stacey.

"Can you give me those directions?"

"Sure." He repeated them, and Nancy nodded along. "Did you get all that?" he asked after he finished.

"I think so. But can you still tell me the address?"

"If you follow the directions, you'll get here with no problem. Do you know why I tell a lot of jokes? Because I'm hoping that the day comes when someone tells me a joke and it turns out to be one of the ones I made up. I want it to go all the way around the world, maybe get a few improvements along the way. Because you know what, Nancy? No one tells a joke the same way."

Outside, interstate mile markers passed the car, the numbers going down, down, down, approaching zero.

"I guess I never thought of it that way," Nancy said.

"I think up things no one has ever thought of before," said Stacey. "I like you, Nancy."

"I like you too," said Nancy, her tone sincere.

"If it makes you feel better, then I'll give you the address." After he gave it to her, she recited it back, gesturing for Steve to input it into the GPS.

"But you'll remember the directions?" asked Stacey.

On the car's console, a blue light formed, showing the way to go.

"I will," said Nancy, her eyes tracking the blue line.

"I might quiz you when you get here," Stacey said. Then he laughed in a loud, boisterous way.

Nancy politely returned the laughter while Steve mimed hanging himself with a rope. Then he signaled for her to hang up.

"I have to go, Stacey," she said. "It was good talking to you."

"It was good talking to you, and it'll be even *better* seeing you. When I do, you can say hi to my parents, and then we can go get something to eat at Taco Bob's. My treat."

Nancy's eyes flashed to the back seat, where they kept a large cooler, a blue and white coffin that stored their supply of water and soda. "We'll have to clear out the back seat first."

"Oh, I'll have to drive," said Stacey, laughing. "Unless you have a really big back seat."

Eventually, after hearing the directions two more times, Nancy ended the call and handed Steve his phone. Then they followed the blue line to Stacey's house.

2

"That Was a Different Scratchy"

The sky darkened, and a few raindrops began to fall just as they reached their destination. On the way, Steve told Nancy a little more about past visits he paid to Stacey's family, none of them recent, just ancient history now. He told her how they always owned spacious homes in remote locations, always with two or more floors above the basement and containing enough rooms to make them seem like labyrinths. Each room contained something interesting, even the attic. When Nancy asked how Stacey's family could afford such lavish homes, Steve confessed that he had no answer. "My uncle had a good job. With the government, I think, something he landed when he finished his career in the Coast Guard. It was never clear to me."

"How mysterious," Nancy said without conviction.

"I really don't know," he said.

"Or you can't tell me."

"If I did," Steve said, "I'd have to kill you."

Nancy laughed—much the same way she'd laughed at Stacey's quips.

They finally reached the house by following a thin road across a marsh. Distant thunder accompanied their arrival at the house, a tall, sloping structure with few windows that appeared to frown as it leaned into the wind that blew across the marsh. They parked behind a silver BMW and next to a large pickup truck. The way Nancy eyed the vehicles conveyed an understanding that they'd stepped into the presence of money.

They knocked at the front door and waited quietly for someone to answer. Finally, Steve noticed the doorbell. He pointed to it, and Nancy nodded her agreement that he should press it.

From inside the house came the sound of the bell, followed by a loud racket. Barking, the sort of noise that came from a gigantic dog.

Nancy looked at Steve nervously. *Wrong house?* she mouthed silently. He shook his head.

Finally, the door opened, revealing a tiny, wrinkle-faced woman on the other side, a blond wing crowning her head. She stared at them, her expression befuddled. Behind her, the source of the barking appeared—an enormous Tibetan Mastiff, the sort of animal one expected to find guarding an ancient monastery. The top of its head nearly reached the woman's shoulders, making her look all the more slight in stature. Slavering like a fountain, the dog continued to bark but thankfully didn't cross the threshold of the door.

"Aunt Dolly?" said Steve.

The woman stared at him with wide, surprised eyes, the sort of expression normally reserved for an alien visitor appearing from the sky to probe bodies and erase memories.

"It's Steven." Steve elevated his voice so that she could hear him above the dog's barking.

Someone began yelling from inside the house, demanding that the dog shut up. That voice grew louder and louder until another figure appeared next to Aunt Dolly.

"Uncle Reuben?" said Steve. "It's Steven."

Steve and Nancy huddled close to each other on the front stoop, awaiting a welcome. Uncle Reuben wore a cap, the kind worn by taxi drivers, and it hung low on his brow, just above a pair of rapidly blinking eyes.

"Steven?" said Uncle Reuben. "Weren't you just here?"

"Yes, it's Steven. And no, we're arriving for the first time."

"I remember this happening already." Uncle Reuben blinked several more times. "How are you?"

"Good."

Steven and Nancy waited for someone to invite them in, standing there like traveling salespeople, like Jehovah's Witnesses. Another ten seconds went by without anyone saying anything. Even the dog stopped barking. Finally, Nancy drew a breath and held out her hand. She introduced herself.

"I'm sorry," Steve said. "It's just been so long. Did Stacey tell you we were dropping by?"

The dog started barking again. Uncle Reuben looked down at the animal and yelled a sequence of profanities at it.

"You'd better pet her," said Aunt Dolly, her voice rising above the noise.

Steve and Nancy stared at the enormous dog on the other side of the threshold. Adding to the din, Uncle Reuben continued to scream at the dog. "Shut up! Goddammit, shut up, shut up, shut up, shut, shut, shut, shut up!"

"She likes petting," Aunt Dolly said. "Come in and pet her or she'll keep barking."

Finally, Steve took a nervous step through the doorway.

Nancy hesitated, but she followed him inside and watched as he touched the barking dog's head. Frothing drool ran from the dog's mouth, but as if by magic, the instant it felt Steve's hand, the barking stopped, along with Uncle Reuben's yelling.

"This is Scratchy," said Uncle Reuben at a volume so normal that it startled everyone. One would never know he was yelling like a madman a second before.

Steve stopped petting the mastiff for a moment, and it immediately began barking again. Before Uncle Reuben could start yelling, Steve recommenced the petting, and the animal quieted.

"I think you had Scratchy the last time I was here," said Steve. "She must be really old."

"Oh, no, that was a different Scratchy," Aunt Dolly said. "That one went missing. Ran away."

"This is the fifth Scratchy," said Uncle Reuben.

"The fifth?" asked Nancy. "You've had five mastiffs?"

Uncle Reuben's eyes turned up toward the brim of his cap as he did a silent count. "Seven, actually."

"Seven? That seems impossible," said Steven. "I only remember the one." He didn't stop petting the animal, which slavered happily and remained quiet. It acted as if it had waited all its life for someone to pet it the way Steve did.

"Seven," Uncle Reuben said. As everyone watched Steve pet the dog, he seemed to rethink it. "Eight."

Aunt Dolly stared at Nancy.

"I'm Nancy," Nancy said. She held out her hand again, but Aunt Dolly didn't appear to notice.

"Do you have to use the bathroom?" Aunt Dolly asked Nancy.

"Actually, yes, I do." Nancy glanced nervous from Aunt Dolly to Steve and then back to Aunt Dolly.

"I have to show you where to do that," said Aunt Dolly. "I can always tell when people have to use the bathroom."

They followed Aunt Dolly through an enormous living room with a high ceiling and a large picture window that looked out upon the marsh they had crossed to reach the house. The furniture and layout of the house indicated worn opulence, with Scratchy's smell permeating everything. Dust hung in the air, along with a hint of decay. Steve tried to pet the dog as they walked, but when remaining hunched over proved difficult, he took a chance and stopped. He breathed a sigh of relief when the dog didn't resume barking. Instead, the dog walked beside him as they proceeded in a single file line toward the bathroom. On the walls hung several paintings of dogs, all of them Tibetan Mastiffs like Scratchy, including a grand portrait fit for royalty hanging over the fireplace.

Aunt Dolly moved with a stooped gait, and they all needed to match her short steps in order to allow her to stay in the lead. That gave time for Nancy to scan the once-lush furnishings of the house, and she conveyed several compliments, which went unanswered. Finally, Aunt Dolly stopped outside a door in a short hallway that ran between the kitchen and a large staircase. "Here's the bathroom," she said.

Everyone stood back so that Nancy could get past them. She entered the bathroom, her eyes avoiding them as she shut the door behind her. Then they all waited in the hallway, Uncle Reuben, Aunt Dolly, Steve, and Scratchy, everyone remaining mute and nothing to mask the sound of Nancy urinating. When Nancy finished, Aunt Dolly led them all through the kitchen and into another living room, where a TV ran reports of expected rain. There, each took a seat on one of the two sagging sofas.

"Is Stacey here?" Steve asked. "We told him we were coming."

Nancy nodded. "I'm looking forward to meeting Stacey."

"You are?" asked Aunt Dolly. "What have you heard?"

Steve shifted in his seat. "I told her a few things. Like how when we were kids, I helped him out one time with his paper route."

Nancy nodded along and pretended Steve really had told her about a paper route.

"Is he still delivering papers?" Steve asked.

"Oh, no," Uncle Reuben said. "He doesn't do that. He works at a convenience store."

Aunt Dolly watched Nancy throughout the conversation. Her wig shifted at some point, revealing a tuft of thin, gray hair. "What have you heard?" she asked again.

But before Nancy could answer, Scratchy started barking again, and without prompting, Steve started petting again, only this time the dog refused to stop, so Uncle Reuben began yelling, the noise increasing in volume, until they heard another voice, one louder than all the rest.

"You're here!"

The noise ceased as they all turned to see a large form filling the entryway behind them.

3

"What's the Jungle Room?"

Despite his imposing size, a polo shirt hung loosely from Stacey's body, green in color and damp from perspiration. Though over forty, a thick, boyish mop of blond hair covered his forehead, glistening wet just like his face. His chest rose and fell as he gazed upon his visitors, his small eyes buried deep within the reddening flesh of his cheeks.

"Steven!" he said as he took a lumbering step into the room, the heft of his body testing unsteady knees. Steve and Nancy rose from the sofa, while Uncle Reuben and Aunt Dolly became engrossed in the weather report. Stacey wrapped his arms around Steve and squeezed. "I've been so excited to see you that I canceled my doctor's appointment." He finally let go of Steve and regarded Nancy, but he didn't hug her. "Did you already know that I didn't have to work today? Is that why you chose today to visit?"

Nancy and Steve searched one another's face for an answer. Finally, Nancy's expression brightened. "Oh, today's a holiday. I completely forgot." She turned to everyone in the room, even Uncle Reuben and Aunt Dolly, who remained fixated on the television. "It's June 19th. Juneteenth."

"Is it?" asked Stacey, his smile revealing perfectly white teeth.

"Yes." Nancy went on to explain how the new federal holiday commemorated the date on which the former slaves in Galveston, Texas, learned of the Emancipation Proclamation. Her voice competed with reports of impending thunderstorms. As her monologue continued, Stacey's eyes drifted back to Steve, and his smile grew even wider.

When Nancy finished, Steve said, "This is Nancy. She taught college for a while up north. Literature courses, mainly. She liked to assign readings by Frederick Douglass."

Stacey nodded. "I didn't vote for Obama. Listen, Steven, I want you to see my room. Remember how we used to look at comic books together? I have even more now."

From his seat on the sofa, Uncle Reuben broke into the conversation. "You're bringing rain with you."

"I hope not." Nancy looked at Stacey. "Did you know that Steven writes for a living?"

Stacey managed to widen his small eyes. "No! Really? Comic books?"

Steve shook his head and smiled sheepishly, the way he always did when someone mentioned his writing. "Mostly technically manuals. Nothing exciting."

"Technical books? That's wonderful. Do you have any of your books with you?"

"As a matter of fact, I do. We just left a convention. But it's boring stuff, really."

"But you write about factual things. Like how to put things together?"

"Sure. Sometimes." Steve looked at Nancy and laughed nervously.

"That's perfect. I know someone who's putting something together. Something wonderful. It's a grand venture, the kind of thing needed in these dark times. These *are* dark times, wouldn't you agree?"

Steve responded the way people always do when presented with such a question. He frowned and said that yes, they certainly lived in dark times.

Reassured, Stacey nodded. "I'm glad to hear you say that. There are so many stupid, brainwashed people everywhere, but wait until you get a look at what my friend is doing. I'll bet he'd like to read one of your books. Maybe he'll like it and let you write about his project. I want to read your book too, so I'll get a copy from you later. Don't worry, I'll pay for it. Or maybe we can trade. I have a lot of stuff in my room." The rapid succession of ideas took its toll on Stacey. His mouth could hardly keep up with what he wanted to say. Moisture formed on his brow, creating tiny rivulets that ran down his face. The damp spots on his shirt multiplied.

"Did you just get out of the shower?" asked Nancy.

"*No.*" Stacey spoke this word a little too forcefully, startling Scratchy into barking again. Without prompting, Steve petted her until she finally quieted, whereupon the voice of a meteorologist filled the room.

"You hear that?" said Stacey. "A 'weather event' he calls it. They don't even call it 'rain' anymore. That way, no one can accuse them of making wrong predictions. Just try calling them up at the TV station to complain, and they'll deny they said anything about rain. That's all people do today: deny things. It's so bad that you can't even trust weather predictions. Well, *I'm* not going to be brainwashed. But just in case it does rain, we better get started. I'll take you around the island and, later on, buy you lunch at Taco Bob's. Ever been to Taco Bob's?"

They shook their heads.

"Well, you'll love it. My treat."

Nancy looked toward Uncle Reuben and Aunt Dolly, both of them transfixed by the weather report. "Are you coming too?"

If they heard, Stacey didn't give them time to answer. "There isn't any room for them."

"If we move the cooler from the backseat . . ."

But Stacey didn't let Steve finish. "I have bad knees. My doctor says I shouldn't ride in a vehicle driven by someone unfamiliar with my condition." He looked at Nancy. "Did you follow the directions I gave you?"

She smiled. "I sure did."

Stacey narrowed his gaze, his eyes as bright as freshly polished nails. "Did you really?"

"Of course she did," said Steve. "I made sure."

Stacey acted as if he didn't hear him. Instead, he continued to scrutinize Nancy. "When you turned on Holly Rae Avenue, how many lights did you go through before you came to Garcia Boulevard?"

At first, Nancy laughed. Then, after she read Stacey's expression and realized he expected a serious answer, she pursed her lips. Even Uncle Reuben and Aunt Dolly looked away from the TV so that they could hear the answer.

"Three," she said. "No, wait. *Four.* I'm sure it was four."

The two older people returned their attention to the television.

"Four. You're sure it wasn't *three*?" asked Stacey. The perspiration spread across his chest.

"It was four," Nancy said. She looked to Steve for support, but he just shrugged his shoulders, a funny smile on his lips.

"Well, we're going that way to get to Taco Bob's. What do you say we count? It's very important that you follow my directions. With tourist season about to get started, traffic gets crazy, and you can get stuck in it. But before we go, I'll show you where you're sleeping."

Aunt Dolly looked up. "I'll need to show them where they can use the bathroom."

"*Mom!*" Stacey's face grew red. "I'll take care of it." Then he regarded Steve. "You're staying in the Jungle Room."

"What's the Jungle Room?" asked Nancy.

Stacey smiled. "I'll show you."

4

"Are Those Tigers?"

At no time during the drive did Steve and Nancy talk about spending the night or what they would say if an invitation came up. As a result, they floundered helplessly, caught in the gravity of fate. Like meteors doomed to ignite and burn in the earth's atmosphere, they formed a line behind Stacey, with Steve in front of Nancy. Scratchy trailed along behind Nancy, and in the dog's wake, Aunt Dolly and Uncle Reuben shuffled not far behind.

As they walked toward the staircase, they passed more paintings of Tibetan Mastiffs, each painting more regal than the last, though the dogs all looked the same.

"Are these all the past Scratchys?" asked Nancy

"Different artists," said Uncle Reuben, "but they are more or less the same Scratchy."

"Do you keep pictures of family members somewhere else?"

Nancy's question drew Steve's attention. He turned to hear the answer, nearly resulting in a collision between him and Stacey and bringing the whole slow progression to a halt.

"No," Uncle Reuben said. Uncle Reuben's choice of headwear

made it hard to see his eyes, rendering his tone and expression a mystery.

Stacey stopped at the foot of the stairs. He took a deep breath and gripped the banister with his right hand. He stood poised like that for several moments, with everyone queued up behind him, waiting to follow. Finally, he looked over his shoulder at Steve. "I have a surprise to show you later."

"You do?"

"Yes, and when you see it, you'll want to give me one of your books. But I'll buy it from you if you want."

"You don't have to do that," Steve said.

Nancy stood on her toes and looked over Steve at Stacey. "Is the Jungle Room up the stairs?"

Stacey offered no response. From the end of the line came the voice of Aunt Dolly. "Do you need to use the bathroom again? I can usually tell."

"No." Nancy put a little too much emphasis on her answer, and Uncle Reuben scrutinized her with glassy eyes. Nancy looked away. "I just need something to drink." When no one offered her one, she said, "But we brought plenty of water bottles. They're in our cooler." To Steve, she added, "Maybe I'll go down and grab one."

"There's plenty of time later for that later," Stacey said. "You need to see the Jungle Room first."

Whereupon he started up the stairs, a slow process, one requiring frequent stops to take a breath as he used the banister railing to pull himself up one step at a time. Everyone else remained dutifully in line behind him—even Scratchy, who maintained her place behind Nancy, finally refraining from barking.

Finally, after several seconds and half a flight of steps, they reached a small landing where a double door awaited them. Perspiration glistened on Stacey's forehead, cheeks, and neck. "Here it is," he said in between deep breaths. "The Jungle Room." Then he swung open the doors and presented them with a massive room filled with dust and an eclectic array of objects and furniture.

From their vantage point just inside the doorway, they could easily see why they called it "the Jungle Room." Every choice of décor suggested a wild colonialist fantasy, starting with the throw rugs with leopard spots. Even the different shades of green used to paint the walls lent the impression of thick, choking vine growth. Nearly every available flat surface in the enormous room, from dressers to coffee tables, displayed some sort of replica of a giraffe, a zebra, or a lion. Some of the larger, if not quite life-sized replicas sat on the floor itself. On a small table in the back of the room sat an old manual typewriter, looking as sad and lonely as a missionary no one wanted to visit to make their required confession.

But nothing else drew the eye quite like the skeletons.

"Are those tigers?" asked Nancy.

Stacey laughed. "My goodness, no. Tigers are huge. These are just big."

"They look plenty huge to me," Nancy said.

"Mastiffs," Steve said quietly.

Stacey nodded with approval. "Yes, Steven. God, you're smart. I'll bet your books are something."

Hesitating, Steve and Nancy followed Stacey further into the room, where they could better see the skeletons of the dogs, each one displayed in a different fashion. One of them appeared with an arched spine and its head low to the ground, as if tracking a scent. Another stood up straight and alert, at least three feet off the ground, its formidable teeth appearing to grin. Its tail lay detached a few feet away, either fallen off or never affixed in the first place. Still another skeleton lay in a heap, waiting for someone to sort its pieces back together and make it whole once again. All the others looked all or nearly complete and seemed to stalk the group that walked toward the middle of the room.

"Scratchys," said Uncle Reuben.

At the sound of the name, Nancy looked for the living Scratchy. It turned out that the dog never even entered the room. Instead, it sat just outside the threshold of the room, keeping watch on the humans and whining nervously.

"She doesn't seem to like this room," said Nancy.

"That's not true, *Nancy*." The way Stacey spoke her name made Nancy shift nervously. "She's simply not allowed in this room, and she knows it."

"I count nine."

Everyone turned to Steve.

"Nine?" asked Stacey. "Nine what?"

Steve nodded. "Nine dogs here." He looked at Uncle Reuben. "You said there were eight Scratchys."

Uncle Reuben blinked several times. "I did?"

"Nine indeed," Stacey said. With his hands on his hips, he surveyed the room and its skeletons. "Nine. Plus the one outside makes ten. How about that."

Aunt Dolly tapped Nancy on the shoulder. "Let me show you the bathroom." She opened a set of louvered doors to their right, revealing a sink and bathtub. "The shower works," said Aunt Dolly.

"Fantastic," Nancy said. Aunt Dolly moved aside so she could step in, but Nancy waved her off with a forced smile. "I really just want something to drink. I'm parched."

"Taco Bob's has a fine selection of beverages," Stacey said. "We should get going. I want to show you around town before the rain starts."

Nancy started to answer, but Steve spoke first. "I'm starved. It's been a long trip, hasn't it, Nancy?"

Nancy nodded.

"Let's get started," said Stacey.

5

"Do You KnowThose Tests on the Internet Designed to Make Sure You're Human?"

"Did you reconstruct all those skeletons by yourself?" asked Nancy from the back seat.

In the front seat, Steve sat next to Stacey, who drove aggressively at high speeds, frequently braking, even without any discernible impediment in the truck's way. His method of driving caused them all to lurch forward several times, especially Nancy, thanks to a broken seat belt. At one point, a sudden stop nearly hurled her into the front seat. Steven held himself secure by clutching the handle above the door, but even with a functioning seat belt, he still struggled to keep his head from striking the dashboard with each pump of the brakes. Facing forward, he couldn't see the dour expression on Nancy's face.

Earlier, as they walked toward the vehicle, she touched Steve's wrist and indicated he should lean close to her so she could whisper. "I don't want to stay in that room."

Steve glanced back toward the door, where Stacey paused to lock a series of deadbolts, even though Aunt Dolly and Uncle Reuben would remain behind. Taking deep, gasping breaths, Stacey carefully navigated the front steps leading to where Nancy and Steve waited in the driveway.

"We'll play it by ear," said Steve. "We ought to eat lunch with him at least. I really am starved."

"You promise?"

Steve glance back toward Stacey, who stopped on the middle step in an attempt to catch his breath again.

"Pinky promise," he said. "We won't stay any longer than we need to." With these words, he extended his pinky so she could grab it with her own.

Neither of them talked or even thought about food once they became familiar with Stacey's pattern of driving. In response to Nancy's question about the skeletons, Stacey nodded energetically. "A craft I developed while working with a friend. I want to introduce him to you. Steven, what do you write again?"

"Technical manuals," Steve said.

"Couldn't break into comic books?"

"I never really tried." He turned to regard Nancy. "It was a dream of mine to write comics when I was a kid."

Stacey nodded along with this information like someone who has known a secret for many years and can now share it with the world. "We used to look at comics when you'd visit. Remember that?"

Instead of answering, Steve glanced back at Nancy. Her face also bore a smile, one that revealed worry lines around her mouth and eyes. "I didn't know that about you, Steven."

The name caused Steve to raise an eyebrow. She never called

him by his proper name. Always just Steve.

"Oh, sure," Stacey said. The truck lurched twice under his heavy foot. "We would sit in my room for hours with a stack of Gold Key comics between us. You remember Doctor Spektor, Steven?"

Steve nodded as the truck's movement caused his shoulder to strike the passenger door.

"Later, I'd like you to come up to my room at the top of the stairs. I still have all those old comics," said Stacey.

"Sure, I'll do that."

Stacey expressed his excitement by pumping the brake pedal. This time, Steve managed to hold himself steady, but Nancy nearly flew into the front seat.

"Stacey," she said, "can you go a little easier on the braking?"

"Why, certainly. But we'll be stopping soon. There's a thrift shop nearby, and I want to take Steven there."

"I'd really like to see the water," said Nancy. "Any chance you can take us somewhere like that? I've never been here. Right, Steven?"

This time, Steve responded to her use of that name with an arched eyebrow. If Stacey noticed, he failed to mention it. Instead, the truck came to a rough stop at a yellow light.

"*One*," Stacey said.

"Pardon?" asked Steve.

Instead of answering, Stacey adjusted his mirror so that he could see Nancy's reflection. "What is it you do? Teach school, correct?"

"No," she said.

Before she could say more, Steve said, "Nancy's a photographer."

"That's interesting. You said she was a teacher."

"No," said Steve, "I never said that."

Nancy touched Steve's shoulder. "You mentioned that I taught college for a little while. But I don't do that anymore. I found I was at my happiest by doing photography."

"Huh. Interesting. Steven? Do you think you're at your happiest by writing . . . what was it?"

"Technical manuals," Steve said.

"Right. Do you think you're as happy as Nancy by writing technical manuals instead of comic books?" As he spoke, the light turned green. The truck accelerated quickly with the tires squealing. The erratic driving resumed with more constant braking.

Steve struggled to settle himself before answering. "I don't know. The comics were kid stuff, I suppose."

"I suppose so too," said Stacey. "I do have an idea for a technical manual. I'll tell you about it later, and before you go, I'll buy one of your books."

"They're not the sort of thing someone buys in a bookstore," said Nancy. "Hey, Stacey? Don't forget the braking."

Once more, Stacey used his mirror to scrutinize Nancy's reflection. "What is it you photograph, Nancy? Are your pictures in a book?"

"I take pictures of different objects. Things like bicycles, stairs, and trees."

Steve said, "Do you know those tests on the Internet designed to make sure you're human? The ones that, before logging onto a website, you get a grid of pictures, and you're supposed to click on the ones that show a bicycle?" Steve waited a beat for Stacey to answer. When none came, he said, "Those are often Nancy's pictures."

"I haven't seen any of those," Stacey said.

"Surely you have. Everyone's seen my photos," Nancy said. "I'll show you later, if you want."

Instead of answering, Stacey came to another abrupt stop at a traffic light. "*Two*," he said.

"If you want to, sure, but not while you're driving," said Nancy. She glanced in Steve's direction, but he failed to notice.

"Maybe, maybe," Stacey said, his voice trailing off as they waited for the light to turn. When it did, the truck took a hard turn and jostled into an unpaved alley. "First, let's go into the thrift store. It's right here."

6

"Maybe It's Just a Sideshow"

After hitting the curb with the front tire, Stacey drove toward a low, flat building with windows boarded by plywood. A sign announced the business housed within the building, but time and weather faded the lettering so that only one word remained visible: *Treasures*. Instead of parking in the front, Stacey drove to the rear, where he brought the truck to a hard stop next to a dumpster overflowing with garbage. He pointed toward the building, where a set of heavy rubber flaps hung over an entrance that looked intended for deliveries and donations.

"We're going in there," Stacey said. "Steven, will you help me?"

It turned out that Stacey needed assistance getting out of the driver's seat. While Steve used both of his arms and all his strength to do as Stacey asked, Nancy stood with her hands on her hips, regarding the store.

Now standing and sweating from both physical exertion and the humidity, Stacey waved for Steven to join him at the truck's rear. Between deep gulps of air, Stacey said, "I don't think

28

Nancy likes me."

"Oh!" Steve's eyes darted to where Nancy stood, her position unchanged. She gave no sign she heard the conversation. "I can guarantee you that isn't the case. Nancy likes everyone. That's the kind of person she is."

Stacey nodded his understanding. Then he said, "Do you think I'm a racist, Steven?"

Steve's brow furrowed. "No, not at all."

Stacey persisted. "Do you think I'm a white supremacist?"

"Jesus. Of course not."

Stacey nodded. "That's good. Because I have proof that such labels are meaningless and stupid. I'll show you later. In the meantime, help me with these."

Along with several industrial-sized bags, two cardboard boxes sat in the bed of the truck. Peeling, misaligned tape secured the lids to the boxes and provided little aid to their crumpled corners. It looked as though something very heavy lay atop them at some point. At Stacey's direction, Steve picked up one of the boxes, but he nearly dropped it when a cockroach ran across his hand. A second later, Stacey placed the other box on top of the first one, leaving his own hands free.

"Thank you," Stacey said. "You go ahead." He pointed toward a door next to the wider entrance. "Just go on in. It'll be open."

Steve nodded and began to walk, his arms overloaded with the boxes. Behind him, Stacey limped slowly, his breathing raspy and his perspiration pouring more heavily than ever before. Ahead of Steve, Nancy paused and waited for him just outside the flap.

"This is making me uncomfortable. Not just his insane driving. Everything." She spoke softly and with her back to Stacey. "What's in there?" She meant the boxes.

"Don't know. Stuff he's donating, I guess."

"It looks heavy. What about your back?"

"I'm fine. He'd never make it here with them. I'm worried about him. He looks like he might have a heart attack at any second."

As one, they turned toward Stacey, who slowed his pace even more to step around a puddle. He waved at them. "Go on in. Look around. I'm almost there."

"If he keeps driving the way he does," Nancy said, "I'll have a heart attack. Tell him it hurts your back."

"My back is fine."

"Tell him. He obviously likes you. Loves you, in fact. I'm not sure he feels anything but animosity for me."

"That's not true. Stacey likes everyone. Besides, you're very loveable."

They stopped talking as Stacey drew close enough to hear them. "Go on," he said, waving them along. "I'm almost there."

Nancy nodded and waved before she passed through the flaps. Steve did what Stacey wanted and tried using the smaller door, though having his hands occupied made it difficult. Not only that, but the doorknob hung loosely and threatened to fall off entirely.

Finally, just as Stacey appeared behind him, he managed to wiggle it open, granting him passage into a large room packed with similar boxes, all stacked haphazardly.

"Go on in, go on, go on," Stacey said between great gulps of air.

The stacks formed a precarious, uneven path with so many turns that Steve couldn't see where it led. Sighing, he clutched the boxes and began walking. The pathway became so narrow at times that he needed to walk sideways with his elbows tucked down. He didn't know how Stacey, with a body the size of a small bull, could possibly make it through himself. In fact, when he looked over his shoulder, he saw no sign of his cousin, leaving him no choice but to forge onward. Eventually, the path of boxes gradually widened into what looked like a kind of work area, complete with a carpenter's bench covered with tools and several old radios with their guts spilling out. On a tack board over the bench, someone had pinned a *Let's Go Brandon!* sign. Dust motes filled the air, and smells of rot, mold, and stale tobacco permeated everything.

He almost didn't notice the woman. "Can I help you?" she said in a tone clearly meant to convey that she wouldn't help him at all, not for all the money in the world.

Her presence caused Steve to stammer until he found the right words. "I'm with Stacey." He held up the sagging boxes for emphasis. "He sent me with these."

The woman sniffed and stepped forward, a tube of glue in her hand. From a distance, her ponytail and cut-off shorts made her look youthful, but that impression changed as she closed the distance between them. Wrinkles above her lip indicated a heavy smoker, while the dark spots on her teeth and her receding gums suggested other habits. The closer she came, the more the air itself seemed to ripple with loathing and rank exhalation. She didn't offer to relieve him of the boxes, but her thin, veiny arms didn't look up to the task. She wore a pink tank top emblazoned with letters that spelled out *Tell Me Why I Should Give a Fuck.* After sizing up Steve, she pointed toward the carpenter's bench. "Put those over there."

Steve nodded. With no clear space on the bench, the boxes sat unevenly, and the top one started to slide off. The woman clucked with irritation, but Steve managed to keep the box from falling. His hand came away sticky. Whether from the box or the carpenter's bench, he couldn't tell.

Steve and the woman stared at each other.

Finally, the woman said, "You want a receipt? Or you waiting to see if I'll suck your dick?"

Steve stood frozen. They stared at one another, waiting to see what the other would do.

"Does Stacey normally get one?" Steve finally said.

She arched a scarred eyebrow, waiting for clarification.

"A receipt," Steve clarified.

Her expression hardened even more as she reached for a pad, and using a pencil, she scribbled something. Steve held fast as she walked up to him, her hips swinging even as she maintained the severe expression. Only a few inches separated them when she finally stopped, close enough for them to count pores on each other's skin. Without breaking eye contact, the woman slid the paper down the front of Steve's pants before abruptly turning back to the work bench.

Withdrawing the crumpled paper from his waist band, Steve mumbled an awkward "Thank you." He started back in the direction that brought him here.

Without casting him another glance, the woman snapped her fingers. "Not that way. I don't like stupid fucks coming into my work area. Go that way." She pointed toward the corner of the room where a Confederate flag hung lengthwise down the wall.

Steve nodded in obeisance. As he walked toward the flag, he straightened out the receipt so he could see what she'd written. Nothing about the contents of the box or its monetary value. Just words: *i would of sucked your cock if you wasn't a fucking asshole.*

It turned out that the flag served as a curtain that covered the entrance into another part of the building, one only slightly more sanitary and organized in appearance. Merchandise for sale, by the looks of it, mostly furniture and cheap knickknacks bearing price tags. Bookshelves lined one side of the room, where Stacey stood alongside a gray-haired man. Steve stuffed the woman's note into his front pocket and joined them.

"I thought you were behind me," Steve said. "Did you see what happened back there?"

Stacey smiled. "You must've met Pepper! Did you like her? I've been wanting to introduce her to you for so long. She's a creative genius, a lot like you are. I can only imagine the kind of juices that would flow between you two. It's a shame you're already married; it really is."

Steve nodded as he studied their surroundings. He avoided looking directly at Stacey or his companion, though Stacey appeared unbothered by his distraction. Instead, Stacey turned to the third man. "Jaspar, this is the cousin I told you about, Steven. Steven, this is Jaspar. I know I said that Pepper is a creative genius, but Jaspar is the true mastermind, a genuine scholar. He knows more about everything than anyone I know. He's better than any book you can buy."

Jaspar and Steve considered one another quietly as Stacey talked. With his gray hair and wrinkled jowls, Jaspar looked anywhere between sixty and eighty, though the weight of those years did not bow him or make him look physically inferior or weak in any way. He wore tiny glasses which followed Steve's gaze across the room toward a sign that said *This Way to the Miscegenation Museum. Free Admission.*

"Jaspar's the guiding hand behind the museum. He's also in charge of all the books and comics," Stacey said. "What is it you call yourself, Jaspar?"

"An antiquarian," Jaspar said, his attention honed on Steve. "An honor to meet you." He spoke from the side of his mouth like a stroke victim. Nothing about him seemed feeble, however. He held out a vein-lined hand, and after hesitating, Steve accepted it, leaving some of the sticky residue from box on the palm on his new acquaintance. Jaspar showed no evidence that it bothered him.

"Steve's a writer," Stacey said.

"You don't say. And what does he write?"

"Well, he doesn't write comics, even though I think he should. He loves them, though, almost as much as I do. Steven, we've been saving some Gold Key titles for you."

But Steve's attention continued to wander. "Where's Nancy?"

"Nancy?" said Stacey, as though he'd never before heard the name. "Oh, I think she's in the museum."

"She did not pay," Jaspar said, still speaking from the side of his mouth. The round glasses made him look calculating and mean.

"It says free admission," Steve said.

"With purchase," said Jaspar.

Steve didn't look at the sign for verification. Instead, he walked in the direction indicated by the sign and found himself facing yet another curtain, this one made of heavy black felt. The paper sign affixed to this curtain said *Entrance.* Without purchasing anything himself, Steve pushed aside the curtain and stepped inside the museum.

Behind the curtain, he faced an all-consuming darkness. Apparently, the curtain's function went beyond shielding the museum from nonpaying eyes. It also provided an effect that became evident when Steve took a hesitant step forward, activating a hidden sensor that caused a blue light bulb to flare, illuminating the museum's first display.

At first, he thought he'd come face to face with another dog skeleton, but this one stood upright like a human. The sight of it caused him to call out Nancy's name. Scampering feet came in response, and soon, Nancy's face appeared in the blue light, her eyes wide, her expression dour.

"You see the face?" she whispered.

Steve squinted, seeing what she meant.

Not a dog skeleton at all but rather that of a misshapen child. Only, the skull adorning the top of the bone structure didn't belong to a human being, its features indicating something more canine in nature. The sign next to it identified it as a *dog person* and listed faraway continents where one could find such a creature.

"There's more that way," Nancy said, pointing, "and they get more disturbing. Like they're trying to imagine different ways you can fuse humans and animals." She described some of these displays, including what looked like the skull of a baby crowning from a taxidermized bear's vulva.

"Maybe it's just a sideshow," Steve said. "A roadside attraction."

"There's nothing here that suggests Barnum and Bailey, Steve. I think these displays are trying to tell a story, one that I can't make sense of. There's something hateful here. There's a word written on one of the displays back there. I don't want to repeat it. It made me sick."

"Are they even real?" Steve meant the bones. He reached out to touch them, but his fingers stopped within a few inches, unable to complete the journey.

"Maybe? I think they are. As for the narrative here, that isn't real. Not unless you look at the world with intolerance." She shook her head. "That word, I can't even say it."

Before Steve could urge her to repeat it, the curtain behind them opened, and the formidable outline of Stacey appeared.

"Ready to go?" he asked.

7

"I'll Bet You Heard of Him: Manimal the Cannibal"

The journey back to Stacey's truck took at least as long as the journey in, largely because Stacey wanted them all to bid farewell to Jaspar.

"You can learn a lot from Jaspar," he said. "A lot more than you can learn from any book." He gestured toward the shelves of moldy hardcovers and water-stained paperbacks. Many of the titles suggested stories of romantic intrigue and adventures in exotic lands.

Jaspar nodded sagely at Stacey's assessment of his genius. At the same time, he regarded Steve and Nancy coldly.

Stacey held up a paper bag for them all to see. "While you were in the museum, I made a purchase."

"A trade," said Jaspar. "Not really a purchase. A purchase you do with money."

"Gold Key comics," said Stacey. *"Grimm's Ghost Stories* and *Doctor Spektor.* You remember those, right, Steven?"

Steve nodded.

"Steven's a *technical writer*," Stacey said to Jaspar. "I was thinking you and he could collaborate. All the things you've taught me should be written down."

"I can impart lessons," said Jaspar.

"Maybe sometime," Steve said.

"Maybe," said Jaspar.

Nancy spoke up. "Stacey? I think my blood sugar is low. Can we get going?"

"Sure, Nancy. Of course."

After final goodbyes to Jaspar and they'd finally buckled themselves into the truck, Stacey turned to Nancy. "I'll bet you think you could drive us home."

Nancy's jaw went slack. "Oh, I don't know about that."

"You don't? Interesting." Stacey started the vehicle, and it soon became clear that the respite at the thrift store had only made his driving worse. Not only did he drive over potholes and take turns at high speeds, but the frequency of his braking only increased, throwing his passengers backwards and forwards constantly.

"Stacey," said Steve, "I don't know if I told you, but I have a back problem."

"A *back problem*?" Stacey sounded stricken, as if he'd just learned about a dire medical diagnosis. "Oh, god, I didn't know. You never had a back problem before you were married to Nancy. *Is it chronic?*"

The roar of the truck's engine rose along with Stacey's voice, and they accelerated quickly, causing both Nancy and Steve to cry out in terror. Within seconds, they flew through a busy intersection, barely missing collisions with the cars crossing from the other direction. As they passed beneath the red light, Stacey shouted, *"Three!"* Then he made a wild left turn that drew them onto a hidden side street, where the truck finally came to a stop.

He turned to gaze at his passengers, who sat frozen in mute horror.

"Did you hear that last number?" he asked quietly, his eyes boring into Nancy.

Nancy said nothing. She worked to regain her breath.

"*Three*," said Stacey, answering his own question, his tone like that of a teacher forced to confront a student's refusal to learn. "That was the *third* traffic light." He shook his finger at her. "You said there were four on that road. Remember? Now I know you didn't follow the directions I gave you."

Nancy's face registered vague recollection. Her eyes welled with tears. "You nearly killed us."

"I want to hear you say it," Stacey said. "All that time I spent giving you accurate directions was a waste. Instead, you put your trust in a cold, soulless machine. Don't you know that this is what *they* want you to do?"

Steve's mouth gaped in frustration. He shook his arms at the clouds hovering overhead outside the truck's windshield. "*They*? Who is *they*?"

Stacey laughed. "I'm confident you know the answer to that question, Steven. You said you knew we lived in dark times. I just want to see if Nancy knows.

Nancy bit her lip. Her voice became soft and even. "I followed your directions. If we went just a little further along that road, we would have come to a fourth traffic light. I'm almost certain."

"*Almost* certain?" Once again, Stacey laughed.

Steve's paroxysm continued. "Who the hell is *they*, Stacey?"

"Think hard, Steven. You already know. If I have to be the one to inform you of a secret cabal controlling the world, then we're all in trouble."

"I don't believe this," Nancy said. She pressed her face into the palms of her hands.

"Communists. Feminists. Scientists. People who use pronouns. I don't need to tell you who else," said Stacey.

"Jesus Christ," Nancy said. Still covering her face, she began rocking back and forth.

"Who you should welcome into your heart, Nancy. Do it fast—before it's too late."

"All right, everyone needs to take a breath," Steve said. "We all need to calm down." He leaned back and tried to touch Nancy, but she pulled away from him. She pressed her hands against her face, muffling a scream of sincere frustration.

"Even the president is part of the cabal," Stacey said.

"Deep breaths. Nancy? Do you have a pill you can take?"

Nancy parted her fingers so she could peer at her husband with a single red-streaked eye. She nodded.

"The secret cabal includes drug users," Stacey said quietly as Nancy reached into her handbag for a pill and popped it into her mouth.

"Enough, Stacey. That's just something she's prescribed for mood swings."

"Don't tell him that," Nancy said, swallowing.

"Pharmaceuticals aren't the answer, Nancy," said Stacey. "People have tried to get me to use drugs, but I always say no."

"I mean it, Stacey. That's enough." Steve looked at Nancy. "Are you okay?"

"I will be," said Stacey.

"Nancy. I was talking to Nancy."

A few tense seconds ticked by before he finally nodded.

"Is she okay?" asked Stacey.

"Yes. We're all okay," said Steve.

"Nancy? I'm sorry if I came on too strong. I really am. I'm just mad that I didn't get to go to my doctor's appointment today. I'm in a lot of pain."

No response from Nancy, her hands now pressed against her ears.

"It's okay, though," Stacey went on. "Jaspar says I can make another appointment soon."

Steve looked away from Nancy to consider what he just heard. "The man at the thrift store is your doctor?"

Stacey nodded. "The best there ever was. You don't need a school for medical knowledge. He comes from a long line of doctors. Their lineage goes back hundreds of years on this island."

Nancy groaned, and they returned their attention to her.

"Nancy?" said Stacey. "You said you take pictures of trees, right? I stopped here for a reason. There's a special tree right over there. Do you see it? It's huge, the biggest in this whole vicinity. It's a very famous tree. What they call a live oak."

Even with her hands pressed against her ears, Nancy heard. She looked toward the windshield.

"Maybe you can take a picture of it to use in one of your internet things," said Stacey.

"I think Nancy wants to—"

But she didn't let Steve finish his sentence. "Sure. I'd like to see the tree." She freed her ears and regarded her husband. "Steven, you'll come with me, won't you?" Instead of waiting for answer, Nancy climbed out of the truck and slammed the door closed behind her.

"I'll wait here," Stacey said. He rolled down his window and turned off his engine. Instantly, he began to sweat.

Nancy moved quickly, requiring Steve to walk briskly to

catch up. He finally reached her under the tree's branches, which spread majestically against the overcast sky. Enormous roots jutted from the soil, requiring careful steps so as not to fall to the ground.

Nancy pressed her hand against the trunk of the tree.

Steve stood behind her and looked up at the canopy of leaves. "It must be over four hundred years old." Tiny droplets of moisture landed on his face.

Nancy kept her back to him. "I wish you would be careful what you say."

"The pill thing? I'm glad you had one."

"That's not what I meant. It wasn't necessary to tell him about my medication."

"You needed one."

"I was fine."

"You do seem fine now."

"I was fine before. Look, I tried calling some hotels when I was in that . . . that museum. But everything's booked. Tourist season apparently."

"It would be rude to bail on them," Steve said. "I think Stacey's calmed down. We need to give this another go."

Nancy stepped back and held up her phone. She began taking pictures of the tree. Dutifully, Steve took a step back, accustomed to her needing clean shots without people in them.

"Don't bother," she said. "I'm just doing this so he won't suspect we're talking about him."

"It's not like we're conspiring. Let's just get settled and try again. He's family."

"Not my family."

"You need to give him a chance. Give all of them a chance."

Nancy continued to take pictures as she spoke. "That

museum. It was ugly, ugly stuff. Who even uses words like *miscegenation* anymore?" She paused as she noticed how the ground sloped downward beyond the tree, where a series of markers lay spread out against the soil. "Is that a cemetery?"

They found a path they could tread easily and made their way to an area enclosed by a short wrought iron fence. Nancy's impression proved correct—a series of grave markers dotted the area, most of them quite old, with several of them made of wood. "He took us to a cemetery," Nancy said as she opened the gate and stepped forth within its boundaries.

Steve pointed to a sign. "A Gullah cemetery. What's that?"

Nancy crouched so she could capture the scene in photographs. She told him what little she knew: that the Gullah people lived up and down the coast of the Carolinas and how they spoke a kind of Creole language heavily influenced by their African ancestors. "I've never seen anything like this. I'm a bit in awe. You feel it, don't you? This is a special place. It deserves reverence." Her lips formed into a smile. "I doubt Stacey intended us to see this. It's a happy accident." She continued to snap pictures as she walked amongst the graves, always careful not to walk across any of the graves and show disrespect for the dead. Steve, on the other hand, didn't show the same discretion.

"Watch your feet," she said.

"They don't care. They're dead." He looked at one of the markers. "And they've been that way for a long time. I can't even read the wooden ones."

"I meant you should watch your feet," Nancy said. She pointed toward a mound of freshly turned soil. "You might walk into a hole or something. There's a few places like that, and I'm not strong enough to pull you out. Stacy could, but he might have a heart attack if he walked this far."

From a distance, they could still see the truck, but the opaqueness of the windshield made it impossible to see inside.

"I can feel him watching us," Stacey said.

"It looks like there's a been a fair amount of digging around here," said Steve. He gestured toward one of the graves covered in freshly upturned dirt. "This person didn't die recently. It wasn't even this century."

"Probably an archeological dig. Someone doing research."

As Nancy paused to take pictures of the marker and the dirt, Steve said, "Wouldn't there be something to indicate it? Maybe tape to mark off the area?"

"Maybe. But this area seems isolated. We almost didn't see it."

After failing to arrive at any answers, they walked back to the truck. Before they drew close, Nancy stopped near the tree and pretended to tie her shoe. "Sit in the back with me," she whispered.

"Won't that look weird?"

She hushed him as they resumed walking. At the truck, Nancy opened the rear door behind the passenger seat. She eyed Steve as she closed door behind her. Steve nodded and walked around the rear of the truck, rounding the other items stored in the bed, including two large bags of industrial-strength lime. Without breaking stride, Steve reached into his pocket and took out the crumpled scrap of paper with Pepper's scrawl. Discretely, he let go of it, allowing it to fall to the ground. Then, with a bounce in his step, as if he'd just let go of a great weight, he opened the other rear door and squeezed himself in behind Stacey and next to Nancy.

This new arrangement seemed to leave Stacey at a loss

for words. Thanks to the position of the steering wheel, he struggled to turn his body so he could look at his passengers. Already with limited space, Steve's position became tighter when Stacey pushed his seat back further. He struggled to find a comfortable position for his feet and knees as Stacey finally found the means to turn far enough around to regard them.

"Did you like what you saw?" he asked.

His voice strained, Steve answered for them both. "Yes, very much."

"Did you get some good pictures, Nancy?"

"Yes," she said.

"The kind that you can sell to . . . what are they?"

"Authentication services. Yes."

The truck remained parked. Despite the looming storm clouds, the air remained still.

"I saw you taking pictures of the graves," said Stacey. His body remained contorted so he could see them. "Will you sell those pictures too?"

"I took those for me," Nancy said. "You know what kind of cemetery that is, don't you? A Gullah cemetery."

She paused for a response, but Stacey said nothing. Sweat poured down his brow like a waterfall.

"They're unique, actually," Nancy said. "The Gullah people. Their dialect, their history, their struggle. You can feel the importance of ancestry here, their connection to the past."

"You know all about them, I guess," said Stacey.

"Not everything. But I can feel how it's a special place. I'll bet it's a good place for reflection, to think about history and what people went through in order to survive hatred and bigotry."

Stacey turned forward and started the truck. His seat remained pushed all the way back as he put the truck into gear, forcing Steve to fidget about, trying to relieve himself of discomfort. Eventually, the truck began rolling in the direction of the main road. Stacey's method of driving proved more restrained this time, with less braking. He even seemed to avoid uneven sections of road.

The smoother ride loosened Nancy's tongue. She went on to describe what she might do with the photos, maybe assemble them into a visual essay about how people had a duty to remember the suffering that went into building the nation. For the first time in a while, she smiled at Steve, and he smiled back as she suggested that maybe he could take a break from his technical writing to do this project with her. Perhaps they could make a future visit and research the families buried in the cemetery, even search out their living descendants for interviews.

Nancy only stopped talking when Stacey interrupted.

"Steven, do you remember the last time you rode in a backseat while I drove?"

The smile that formed on Steve's face moments ago froze into something strange and sheepish. "I can't say that I do," he said.

"Go on, take a guess," Stacey said. He adjusted the rearview mirror so he could see Steve and Steve could see him. Nancy listened.

Steve shook his head. "I really can't remember." Nancy watched as he repeated those words her. "I really can't."

Stacey said, "I'll give you a hint: Carla."

Nancy nudged Steve with her elbow. "Who's Carla?"

Steve's lip fluttered. He grew pale.

"Don't tell me you don't remember Carla," Stacey said. Up ahead, a traffic signal turned red, but instead of stopping, the truck accelerated and flew through it to a chorus of honking horns, violating yet another traffic law.

"*Four,*" said Nancy as the traffic signal and angry motorists faded in the distance.

"What's that?" Stacey turned suddenly and pressed the brake, the movement causing Steve and Nancy to flail about the rear seat. But Steve took the worst of it. The abrupt movement crushed his face and shoulder against the front seat, and he cried out in pain.

The sound of pain caused Stacey's expression to twist in agony. "Oh, dear sweet lord of all creation. God in heaven, no. *I forgot all about your back!*"

"It's okay." But the way Steve's voice croaked suggested otherwise.

"Does it hurt? Well, of course it does. I feel terrible. You know, I have a man who can provide some immediate relief for that pain."

Nancy's eyes flared with energy. "That was the fourth traffic light back there."

"What was?" Stacey's voice dripped with annoyance as he swung into the parking lot of a convenience store. True to form, the wheels struck the curb, causing his passengers to flounce about once more.

"The traffic light you flew through like a goddamn maniac," Nancy said as she righted herself. "That was the fourth one." She drew a breath. "I was right."

The truck parked alongside a metal bar used for locking bicycles. Stacey kept the engine idling as he turned the rearview mirror in her direction. "There's no reason for that kind of language, Nancy. I assure you I don't know what you mean."

"You made a point of telling me I was wrong about the

number of traffic lights. But I wasn't. That was four." Nancy looked at Steve for confirmation, but her husband could only wince in agony. He still looked very pale.

"Nancy," said Stacey, "I assure you I don't know what you mean. I didn't see a traffic light. Right now, my focus is on Steven, who is, in case you haven't noticed, in a great deal of pain. He's my concern right now, and he should be yours too." He reached back and touched Steve's knee, causing his cousin to wince again. "Steven, this is where I work on weekends. The man I told you about? The one who can provide pain relief? He works here too. Part-time like me, but you're in luck because today's his shift. I'm going to go get him, and everything will be fine. I promise. His name is Leslie. That's how we bonded. We both have names that girls normally have. We're practically twins. You wait here, and I'll be right back."

Out of the truck, Stacey moved toward the entrance of the store with greater speed and urgency than they'd yet seen from him. Nancy waited for him to vanish inside before she said, "I could have used some support a minute ago. You saw that traffic light too, didn't you?"

Steve grunted an unintelligible answer and then winced again.

"What's with you? Does your back really hurt that much?"

"It's nothing," he said. "I probably just need to stand up and stretch.

She studied his features, which continued to look wan and discolored.

"Who's Carla?" she asked.

Before he could answer, the door to the convenience store swung open and Stacey reappeared. He moved with uncharacteristic urgency, rushing forth and pressing his sweating face against Steve's window. Behind him, the door opened again, and out came a giant of a man, his muscled torso squeezed into an employee uniform that looked at least a size too small. His long stride carried him alongside Stacey in just four steps. His head was completely bald, and his body seemed to ripple with engorged muscle. He gazed through the window at Steve with an expressionless face.

Stacey tapped at the window. "Steven, this is the man I told you about. Leslie. He's here to help you."

Nancy leaned across Steve to lock his door. "I think he just needs some pain reliever. Can you go back in and get him something?"

"Nancy? Enough with the pharmaceuticals. You clearly rely too much on them, and that isn't healthy. We'll address that later. We're facing an emergency. Besides, Leslie is all the pain relief you need." Stacey pointed a thumb at the giant standing next to him. "Trust me." He tapped again at the window before remembering he held the keys to the truck in his hand. He clicked the fob button to unlock the door while the man named Leslie stood next to him and cracked his knuckles.

Helpless, Steve offered no resistance as Leslie reached for his arm and pulled him out of the truck. Nancy tried to follow, but Stacey closed the door and leaned against it so she couldn't open it. She shifted in the seat to try her own door, but it turned out that Stacey managed to park with the metal bike stand so close to her door that she couldn't open it wide enough to escape. Powerless to do anything else, she watched as Leslie turned Steve around so that his back faced him. Then he wrapped his gigantic arms around him from behind. Still leaning against the truck door, Stacey began counting down out loud, starting at three. When he reached one, Leslie lifted Steve from the ground.

Relegated to watching, Nancy pressed her hand against the truck's window. The stranger held Steve's body nearly three feet off the ground, his fists pressing into his chest. Steve's face twisted in agony. Leslie held him this way for nearly sixty seconds before finally loosening his grip and letting Steve fall to the pavement in a crumpled heap. Once more, Leslie cracked his knuckles before assuming the position of a prize fighter. He shadow-boxed for a few seconds, his movement remarkably graceful for such a large man, pummeling the air with a choreography of punches as Steve lay motionless at his feet.

Meanwhile, Stacey lifted himself off the truck door and opened it. Leaning against it in horror, Nancy nearly fell out onto the pavement next to Steve.

Stacey said, "I don't have any cash, Nancy. Do you?"

Her eyes as wide as saucers, Nancy gazed down at Steve's unmoving form and said, "Cash?"

Stacey gestured toward Leslie, who continued to shadow box. Near his feet, Steve finally moved, trying to gather enough fortitude to sit upright.

"A tip for Leslie," said Stacey. "Just a few dollars will be fine. He clocked out just so he could do us this favor."

Now sitting on his rump, Steve exhaled and rested his elbow on his knee.

"He deserves a tip," Stacey said as he leaned over the seat. "I wouldn't have my job without him. He's world-famous, you know. He used to be a professional wrestler, the best there ever was. I'll bet you heard of him: Manimal the Cannibal. He'd still be a wrestler if not for a mishap, a pretty awful one. He killed someone—by accident, of course. Everyone thinks wrestling is fake, but it's not. Just ask the dead guy. So, Nancy? How much cash do you have so we can tip him?"

Her gaze vacant, Nancy reached for her handbag and dug out two twenties and a dollar bill. She held out the crumpled bills to Stacey. Stacey flattened the money and whistled as he counted it. He stuffed the dollar into his own pocket and held up the twenties for Leslie's approval. Nodding, Leslie finally stopped boxing so he could reach down and help Steve to his feet. Keeping one arm around Steve, Leslie accepted the money and tucked it into his shirt. Then he used his fingers to mime snapping a picture.

Stacey responded with a thumbs up and returned to Nancy. Reflexively, Nancy opened her handbag again and began fumbling around for more money. But Stacey said, "Your camera. He says two twenties buys a photo."

"A photo?" Her gaze shifted back and forth between Stacey and the enormous man with his arm pressed around her husband. Steve wouldn't look back at her, his eyes squeezed shut as if trying to keep them from flying out of his head because of the pressure of the man's arms. "Oh," Nancy said. She stumbled out of the truck with her phone in her hand, maintaining a safe distance as she snapped a photo of Steve and Leslie, the man formerly known as Manimal the Cannibal.

With that act completed, Leslie withdrew his arm from around Steve. He shook hands with Stacey before walking back toward the door to the convenience store, jabbing the air with his fists the whole way. Without the man's arm to support him, Steve slumped but managed to say on his feet. He walked toward the truck on wobbly knees.

Nancy waited for him and touched his arm when he came close enough. "Are you all right?"

Steve flinched at her touch and drew his arm away. "I'm fine. Never better."

"You're lucky he was here," said Stacey, resuming his seat behind the wheel. "Why don't you ride up front, Steven?"

"Yeah, why don't I?" Steve's voice sounded soft and far away.

It took Steve a few minutes to settle in. Even the slightest movement seemed to cause him pain. With his concentration on how to best position his body, he paid no attention to the others in the truck, not even Nancy. Nancy hugged herself as she sat alone, rocking back and forth.

"I'm glad you're feeling better," Stacey said. "I'm sure we all are." He glanced meaningfully at Nancy as he started the engine and backed out of the parking lot. "It's a shame you couldn't get Leslie to autograph that picture you took. Even now, he has quite a fan base. Do you know people actually send him parts of their body through the mail, hoping he'll video himself eating them? Usually, it's just a finger or a pinky toe, nothing too essential, but one time a woman showed up at his apartment holding her own appendix. To humor her, he fried it up with some butter and garlic in a pan, but she ran off before he could actually take a bite of it. He showed it to me, and it looked diseased anyway. He says that he can tell a person's heritage just from how they smell. Except for babies. They're a lot harder. One time, he thought someone sent him the hand of a baby, but I looked at it and told him it was probably just a small monkey. He's full of interesting stories, and I told him they would make a great biography. Would you be interested in writing it?"

Steve didn't answer. He pressed his hand against his rib cage and stared out the window.

Her face concealed by shadow, Nancy finally stopped rocking.

"Steve? Are you really okay?"

"I'm fine," he said without sounding reassuring.

"Now that we're all comfortable again," said Stacey, "are we ready to talk about Carla?"

8

"You'll Never Get Out of Here in This Weather"

"Steven, I think you should start. Don't you remember that time you sat in the backseat with Carla while I drove?"

Steve's voice came out in a hoarse whisper. "I don't. I really don't."

"If it were me, I'd remember," Stacey said. "You sure were having a good time together. I remember how your hands were everywhere. Even under her shirt." He couldn't suppress a giggle as he pumped the brakes, causing the truck to buck like a bull in coitus.

"So this was a girlfriend," said Nancy flatly.

"Carla was my *sister*," Stacey said.

Stacey refrained from excessive braking as these words floated in the air, buoyant as balloons filled with poisonous gas.

"Your *cousin*," Nancy said, her voice filled with disgust. Her gaze roamed about the cabin of the truck, looking for any place to settle other than Steve. "Your *cousin*," she repeated.

Steve drew in a breath. "Yes, Carla was my cousin." He

gripped the handle over the door so tightly that his fist turned purple. Turning to Stacey, he said, "I don't recall anything like that."

Stacey laughed as he swerved into another lane, causing another driver to honk in frustration. He responded by braking again, forcing the other car to avoid an accident by skidding onto the shoulder of the road. "I'm surprised you don't remember," Stacey said as the sound of more honking faded in the distance behind them. "For me, it was a truly memorable weekend. You know the one I'm talking about, don't you?"

No answer from Steve as Stacey's face went on beaming with the joy of nostalgia and recollection.

Nancy bit her lip, and her brow furrowed in thought. "Where's Carla now? I've never heard her mentioned."

"He *never* mentioned my sister?" Stacey peered over his shoulder at Nancy. "Not even once?"

"No," said Nancy.

"That was a long time ago," Steve said.

"It wasn't *that* long ago."

"We were teenagers. Now we're middle-aged. It's ancient history."

"*Where is Carla now?*" Nancy asked.

Steve leaned over, and even though Stacey sat only a few feet away and well within hearing distance, he whispered, "It's a long story."

"Not *that* long. And it's actually quite funny," Stacey said. "But you know what? I'm hungry, and we've finally arrived at Taco Bob's."

The truck turned off the road and lumbered into a dirt lot. In the center of the lot, well-hidden within a clump of pine trees, sat a decrepit food truck, the words *Fine Tacos* stenciled on its exterior. Next to it sat a canopy so tattered that it barely covered a plastic table with a missing leg and two folding chairs. On a ripped back seat stripped from an old Lincoln sedan sat a wiry man wearing a checkered shirt. He stood up when he saw the truck pull in. As they drew closer, the man limped around to the rear of the food truck and disappeared.

No other vehicles occupied the lot, not even the sedan that went with the lonely car seat, but Stacey still parked several feet away. He turned to Nancy. "While you get the food, I want to talk to Steven. His memory is clearly foggy, and I want to help him remember some things. Here's what I want you to get for us." He recited a long order that included an assortment of tacos and burritos, each one specifically layered, followed by an order of *sopes*. "Did you get all that?" he asked.

"No, I didn't. And this doesn't look appetizing at all. I don't what to eat anything that comes out of that truck."

"Really?" Stacey said. "It's delicious. Trust me, you won't be sorry. I eat here all the time."

Nancy chewed her lower lip. Stacey lowered the windows, allowing in humid air and the smell of distant rain.

Steve stared into nothing, his expression so blank that when he spoke, he appeared surprised by the sound of his own voice. "Listen, Nancy, I'm actually very hungry. I'm sure you are too. This looks perfectly fine." He leaned his head out the open window and gazed toward the sky. "Look at those clouds. The rain is going to start really falling soon." He reached back to touch her knee, but she moved it before he could make contact.

"Fine," she finally said. "But I'm nobody's waitress. Not his. Not yours. Come out with me and we'll get—"

Stacey cut her off by repeating his order. "Will you remember?" he asked her when she finished the long list.

"You won't be far. I have no doubt you'll remind me if I forget anything."

"She's right," Steve said. "She's not our waitress. I'll help her." A groan escaped his lips as he exited the truck and made his way toward the open window of the taco truck. Scowling with disapproval, Nancy joined him. No one appeared at the window to offer service, giving them time to read the menu. "You'd think it would be impossible after all that driving, but I actually am hungry," Steve said with a pained smile.

"You're right—I'm hungry too. But this—"

"Everything will be fine." The smile went away as he pressed a hand against the side of his abdomen. "I think that wrestler bruised one of my ribs. But believe it or not, my back is starting to feel better."

Nancy's mouth trembled as if she might scream instead of getting the right words out. "What's the deal with Carla?" she finally managed to say.

"Ancient history," Steve said. "I can't believe he's bringing it up."

"Did you—god, I can't believe I'm about to ask this, but did you do something incestuous with your cousin? And why is it I've never heard of her?"

"Of course not. No. Not really. I mean, I didn't. You know how things are when you're young and—fuck, I don't know—curious?"

"No, I do not," she said in a strained whisper. *Tell me.*

If Steve had an answer, he didn't have time to share it because Stacey's voice interrupted. "Nancy!" His huge arm extended from the truck's window, waving her over to him. Nancy cursed him under her breath and glared at Steve over her shoulder as she walked back to see what Stacey wanted.

"What?" she said.

"Do you have money to tip him?"

"Tip who? There's *no one* to tip."

"He's just being shy. He'll come out. He can't hide in there forever. Maybe he'll show himself sooner if he knows you'll tip him." Stacey grunted as he raised himself off the seat to rummage in his pocket, an act that required energy and stamina. He began to wheeze, but he finally found what he sought—a dollar bill. He held it out to Nancy. "Please give this to him. With my compliments."

Nancy snatched the crumpled bill and stared at it as she walked back to Steve.

"This is my dollar," she said.

"What?" asked Steve.

Nancy started to say more, but they heard the rear of the truck open, and the man who spirited himself away earlier finally reappeared, now carrying a weighted-down plastic bag in each hand. Closer now, they could better discern his features: short with brown hair and skin worn to dark leather from too much sun. Around his waist, a white apron, and on his head, a hairnet that failed to cover three round, festering scabs in a line across his forehead. It looked as though someone tried to drive large nails into his skull, only he managed to get away before they could finish the job.

"Please," he said as he handed the bags to Nancy, "for Mr. Stacey."

"But we didn't tell you what we wanted."

"Please," the man said, leaving Nancy with no choice but to take the bags. They both contained Styrofoam containers with red and green sauces dripped from their corners. "I know what he likes."

Steve peered into one of the bags and inhaled. "That smells delicious. But what about us?"

"Please," the man said. He wiped his hands on his apron and turned around, disappearing into the truck before Steve and Nancy could so or do anything else.

"Bloody hell," said Nancy.

Meanwhile, Stacey tapped his horn to hurry them along. Once again, Nancy swore as she trudged back toward him with the dripping bag.

"Did you get extra sauce?" asked Stacey as he took it through his open window.

"I didn't even get to place an order for me or Steve."

"Oh, there's plenty here for all of us, but I want extra sauce." He seemed unconcerned about how the contents of the bag leaked through the plastic and dripped onto his pants. For her part, Nancy appeared intent on looking anywhere else. "Didn't you tip him?" he asked.

"With *my* dollar? No. We didn't give him *any* money," said Nancy.

"Does it matter whose dollar it is at this point? His time is money. I'll settle with him for the rest later, but you should at least show him your appreciation."

"Goddammit," she said. She uncrumpled the dollar bill and pushed her way past Steve so she could march back to the food truck. The voices faded behind her, Stacey saying something about the alarming frequency of her swearing, and Steve not defending her, instead commenting on how she never did that at home.

Instead of going to the window designated for ordering, Nancy positioned herself behind the rear door and knocked. After waiting a few seconds, she knocked again, this time more insistently.

Finally, the man wearing the apron appeared. "Please," he said.

She held out the dollar bill for him. "This is all I have, but—"

The man took the money and started to close the door before she could finish speaking. Nancy reacted quickly and used her knee to stop him.

"I don't have any more than that," she said, "but if you take plastic—"

"Plastic? No, no." The man tried again to close the door, but Nancy jammed it with her foot. She held up her hand apologetically.

"Stacey necesita salsa," she said.

The man's face changed, and he stopped trying to push the door closed.

"Tu halbas espanol?"

"Un poco."

The man's hand reached back and reappeared with four packets. He pressed them into her palm and didn't let go. In Spanish, he said, "Tell Mr. Stacey that we've heard nothing from Carlos in days. My abuela, she's very worried for his well-being. She's always afraid he doesn't get enough to eat. Will you tell him, please?"

Before Nancy could ask what he meant, he let go of her hand and quickly closed the food truck's door in her face, this time giving her no chance to try that trick with her foot again. She lingered for a moment before rejoining Steve and Stacey.

She found them enjoying the truck's air conditioning, both of them with Styrofoam containers on their laps, their mouths stuffed with food and lips smeared with grease. The sight of them made her gag even as her stomach growled with hunger.

"Where's the extra sauce?" Stacey asked as she climbed into the back seat.

Only then did she look at the packets in her hand, noticing for the first time that the proprietor gave her more than condiments. In between the packets, he slipped a small cross. An accident maybe?

"Did you get them?" asked Steve with a mouth full of food.

"Yeah." She passed him the sauce packets while keeping the cross out of view. She discretely hid it away in the pocket of her jeans.

"The order's wrong," Stacey said in between bites, the Styrofoam container propped between his belly and the steering wheel.

"I never got to place an order."

"It's all good," said Steve. "Plenty for everyone." He extended one of the containers back to her, the twisting motion causing him to moan softly. "I saved you some rice and beans."

"*My* rice and beans. Nancy, you forgot to tell him I wanted pork."

Steve gestured at tacos he held on his lap. "These are pork asada. Nancy, you going to take the rice and beans, or what?"

Once again, Nancy's stomach growled. She practically snatched the container out of his hand and dug in with a plastic fork. For a few minutes, the truck became silent except for the sound of their eating. Not even the occasional smell of flatulence slowed them down. Before them, the Taco Bob food truck sat like an abandoned derelict. Eventually, Stacey belched and tossed his empty containers out the truck window and onto the ground outside before putting the truck into gear.

His driving made it impossible for Steve and Nancy to continue eating, so they closed the lids of their containers and placed the remainder of their food on the floor. Nevertheless, with their hunger somewhat abated, the mood inside the vehicle at least seemed to improve. For a while, it seemed that no one wanted to resume their earlier conversation. A welcome silence reigned.

Until Nancy said, "That man at the taco truck wanted me to convey a message."

Stacey turned his mirror toward her and kept driving. "You don't say."

"Something about Carlos. I don't know if I understood everything because my Spanish is rusty. But I think his family is worried about him. I think his grandmother wants to know if someone is taking care of him."

"Clearly, your Spanish is lacking," said Stacey. "I don't know anyone named Carlos."

"No," said Nancy, stretching the syllable. "I'm sure he said Carlos."

"If you don't mind me asking, where, pray tell, did you learn Spanish?"

"I had two semesters in college. Plus, I went to the University of Miami, so I got a lot of practice. It's not perfect, but it's serviceable. I know I got the name right and the basic gist of the conversation." She reached into her pocket and touched the small cross. But she refrained from mentioning it in her account.

"Well, you clearly learned an inferior version of an inferior language, because I don't know anyone named Carlos."

"Look," said Steve, "I don't think that we—"

"If I went to college," said Stacey, "I would concentrate on learning important things. Like about the weather." As if on cue, the thunderclouds spoke and a light rain began to fall. "Not the kind of weather the elites would have us believe in, but more like the real, factual things you learn by talking to people with lived experience. Like this business about the planet getting hotter and the oceans rising. No, talk to the people who lived here for generation after generation, and they'll tell you what they've learned with their own eyes and brains. The oceans aren't rising. The land is sinking."

"Sinking," repeated Nancy.

"Look at what the rain is doing. Roads washing out, land flooding. It only does that if the land is sinking. When the heavy stuff happens, you'll be glad you're staying with me over night. I wouldn't be surprised if the whole island is closed off soon. Never fear, though: the Jungle Room is all yours."

"About that," Steve said, "maybe we ought to head back to your house so Nancy and I can get on the road. He pointed over his shoulder at his wife. "Nancy is hypoglycemic. You and I pigged out on everything, and she hardly got a bite." He turned so he and Nancy could look at each other. Nancy met his expression with raised eyebrows.

"Oh, that wasn't enough food for even one person. But don't worry. My mother's making dinner tonight. You'll love it. Home-cooked and everything. The best food on the whole island."

"Not that we'll have much to compare it to," Nancy said. "Maybe Steve and I can explore the island on our own. I mean since we didn't get to see much of it."

"You saw the best parts," said Stacey. "That tree is quite a tourist attraction. Truly historical. You probably guessed how often it was used for hangings."

Nancy stammered before she could speak. *"Hangings?* That was a *hanging tree* you took us to see?"

"Well, not anymore. Not officially. It's one of the ways our nation keeps going backwards. You remember Jaspar, the man you met earlier, don't you?" Stacey went on to describe Jaspar's historical expertise, especially when it came to the turbulent decades following the Civil War, when the aristocratic class sought to preserve the island's natural order and hierarchy by hanging anyone who didn't know their proper place.

"That's horrifying," said Nancy.

"You have to put the facts into context, Nancy. The people who owned the plantations were good people who treated their property well. They invested lots of money into their industries. Then, because of the war, they lost everything. At the very least, they wanted people to recognize them as the rightful stewards of the island. But those agitators and upstarts wanted to take over and spit in their eye. Instead of working hard, they chose to steal and murder. They refused to respect the natural authority of men with superior genes and breeding."

"*Natural authority*. Do you even hear yourself? People who think that way don't deserve respect. I would never give them that. And I don't." Nancy tapped Steve's shoulder. "And Steve doesn't either. Right, Steve?"

Steve waved his arms helplessly. "I think we should stop talking about this." He looked at his cousin. "This kind of thing upsets Nancy."

Stacey shook his head sadly. "Not everyone is meant to be free." He spoke these words slowly, so as not to let their profound truth go unnoticed.

"Would you want to be someone else's property? Stacey, I'm asking you."

Stacey chortled at Nancy's question. "I wish you could stay here longer, Nancy. You could stand to learn a great deal, including why that's a ridiculous question."

"Please," said Steve, "let's talk about something else."

"We never told her about Carla." Stacey pumped the brake in excitement, jostling his passengers. But after enduring all the earlier assaults, Steve and Nancy seemed to hardly notice. "We hardly have any time, though. We're almost back home."

By then, the wind began picking up, and the rain fell with greater intensity. The land around them began to flood, with the prairie leading to Stacey's driveway beginning to look like a small lake. The silence in the truck grew tense as Stacey drove through standing water that reached the bottom of the truck's doors.

"You'll never get out of here in this weather," Stacey said. "Good thing you're staying overnight."

No response from Steve or Nancy as the waves created by the truck's wake rolled restlessly behind them.

9

"Oh, Jesus, the Pickle Jar"

Back at the house, they repeated their ritual with Scratchy. The mastiff's persistent barking stopped only as long as Steve kept petting her, which he sometimes forgot to do, causing the noise to erupt once more, to everyone's irritation. Aunt Dolly and Uncle Reuben still wore their respective headpieces, the hat for Reuben and the wig for Dolly. They seemed not to remember their initial meeting, so Steve had to reintroduce them to Nancy.

"I could use a restroom," Nancy said as they finished their new introductions by the front door.

"I knew you needed to go," Aunt Dolly said.

"But first, I need to get some things from the car," said Nancy, shooting Steve a meaningful look. He responded by saying he would help.

The rain and wind forced Nancy to raise her voice. She stood under the umbrella held by Steve as she opened the trunk of their car and reached for their toiletry bag. "Do you think the car could make it through the water?"

As if the sky could answer, Steve peered up at the clouds. The worsening rain plastered his hair against his forehead.

"If we got stuck, we'd just make our problems worse. We need to tough it out. I'm sorry."

"For the rain? For this trip? For Carla?"

He didn't answer. He took out a duffel bag before closing the trunk. "This umbrella isn't doing much. Let's get back in."

But Nancy hesitated. Steve watched as she reached into the pocket of her jeans and pulled out the cross. She held it up for him to see.

"I don't know what it means," she said, going on to tell him how the man at the food truck gave it to her with the sauce packets.

"Maybe you look like you need religion," Steve said. "Maybe he didn't mean to give it to you. It's awfully small."

"I think he gave it to me for protection."

Now they stood by the front door under an overhang. Steve closed the umbrella and studied her. "Protection from what?"

She looked at the door before leaning closer so she could speak at a lower volume. "You don't think something here is horribly wrong?"

"They're my family."

"Who you're apparently very intimate with."

"Stop that. He was exaggerating. Look, it was that 'museum.' That was unsettling, I know. I'll grant you that. But that's just the people around here. They have different ways of looking at things."

Nancy shook her head. "You're making it sound normal. That wasn't normal at all. I'm pretty sure there were human remains in those exhibits. And it wasn't just that museum; it was *everything*. I watched a man, that cannibal wrestler, *assault* you, for Christ's sake. And then I was forced to *pay* him."

"That may have been money well-spent. He really did help my back." Steve swiveled his hips to prove his point, but when he tried to repeat the movement, his face contorted, and he rubbed his side.

"We should report him to the police. In the meantime, I need to look at your ribs," Nancy said. "He could have broken one." She tried to lift his shirt, but he pushed her hand away.

"I'm fine," he said, "and you're fine. You took a pill, didn't you?"

"Yes, I took a fucking pill."

"Good. But lighten up on the language, okay?"

"Why? Do I sound like an upstart or an agitator?

Steve shook his head. "They're old fashioned. That's all I'm saying." The rain intensified, blowing in at angle that caused them to get wet. "Let's go in," Steve said. "My jeans are getting soaked."

Nancy stopped him with hand on his arm. "Wait. What's the deal with Carla? You're not telling me something."

He rolled his eyes. "Are you really going to make me explain that out here? She's—"

Before he could finish, the door opened to reveal Stacey, his face shining with perspiration. "I was starting to worry you both drowned out here. Come in, won't you? We're all waiting for you."

It turned out that Aunt Dolly really did have a dinner menu planned, one that featured chicken cacciatore. With their stomachs still struggling to digest food prepared in a truck, Steve and Nancy urged her not to go to any trouble on their behalf, but Aunt Dolly regarded them with a glassy stare and said, "I was going to make it anyway. I should have enough for everyone."

"That's nice of you," Nancy said. "I wish I had something to contribute."

"Wine," said Steve. "We have the wine we bought while visiting the Finger Lakes."

Nancy glowered at him. Previously, they discussed enjoying the wine when they had time together alone.

But Aunt Dolly said, "We don't drink wine. We're all on medication."

"That's too bad," Steve said.

"You can have some, though."

"No," said Nancy, "we'll save it. That's fine. Right, Steve?"

"Well, we have wine," Aunt Dolly said. "It's old, but you can have it. Drink it."

Beneath the stairs, she showed them where they stowed a row of dusty bottles, several of them only partially full. Whoever sampled them didn't bother to recork them. Aunt Dolly chose one of the open bottles and poured Steve a glass, but it smelled too much like vinegar for him to drink.

"I'll put it in the sauce," Aunt Dolly said when they both refused it.

The voices on the television discussed a new weather report, one that warned of an apocalyptic amount of rain destined to fall on the area over the next eight hours. Still wearing his hat, Uncle Reuben sat in his chair and absorbed this information with a neutral expression. "I've seen this happen before," he said. Beyond the walls of the house, the water slowly rose.

"It floods here often?" asked Nancy.

"Sure it floods," he said without looking away from the television. "It's an island, isn't it?"

Nancy took out her phone and took a seat on the sectional couch across from Uncle Reuben. He appeared not to notice the way she mashed the buttons and made frustrated noises. "I can't get anything. Steve? How about you?"

But Steve didn't hear. He stood with his back to her in the kitchen, watching Aunt Dolly put the finishing touches on her special dish.

Nancy turned to Uncle Reuben. "Do you have WIFI?"

He looked away from the television and regarded the phone in her hand like he'd never seen one before.

"For what?" he asked.

"I need to look for routes off the island. But I'm not getting a good signal. With the weather getting bad, we probably need to leave sooner. Maybe before dinner."

He turned back to the television. "You'll never make it."

"Still," she said, "maybe I ought to check. Do you have a WIFI network with a password?"

"No."

"Without a password?"

"What is it you need?" This question came from Stacey, who appeared out of nowhere. Instead of a shirt, he wore an oversized towel around his shoulders. His hair looked wet, like he'd just stepped out of the shower. He looked over Nancy's shoulder, trying to see the screen of her phone, but she closed her screen and turned it face down on her thigh.

"I was just asking about the WIFI," said Nancy.

"Oh, we don't have one of those. Like I told you, if you want directions, you should come to me. Don't use the godforsaken GPS."

Those letters seemed capture Uncle Reuben's attention. He looked away from the television like he'd just noticed Nancy for the first time. "What is it you've got there?"

She held up her phone. "I'm just looking for available routes."

"Using GPS?"

Nancy nodded. Even though Stacey loomed behind her, she asked about the WIFI again. Uncle Reuben looked at Stacey briefly before answering that no, they didn't have WIFI. "But you know, I worked on the development of GPS. They told you that, right?"

Having overheard from the kitchen, Steve entered the room holding two stemmed glasses with amber liquid. He held one of them out to Nancy. "Brandy," Steve said, reading the question in her eyes. "It's fine." She nodded but watched Steve take a sip before trying it herself. "I didn't know that about GPS."

"It stands for Global Positioning System," Uncle Reuben said, even though no one asked or cared.

Nancy made room for Steve to sit. The sofa sunk low beneath their combined weight. He tried to position his free arm around her but gave up when she leaned away from him. Besides, Scratchy sat near his feet and resumed her barking, so Steve needed to focus on her instead. Once she quieted, he said, "Uncle Reuben used to work for an intelligence agency when the family lived near Washington." Then he added in a faux whisper, *But we aren't supposed to know that.*

"No." Uncle Reuben looked mystified. "You're not supposed to know that at all."

"We used to joke about how often we'd call up and Aunt Dolly would say you couldn't talk because you were in Pennsylvania. We finally figured out that was code for some kind of covert government work. 'Reuben is in Pennsylvania,' she'd say, and we'd hang up the phone and speculate that you'd gone to Moscow or London for some kind of espionage."

"I *was* in Pennsylvania," said Uncle Reuben.

Only Steve laughed at first. After a moment's hesitation,

Nancy laughed nervously, but she stopped when Uncle Reuben failed to acknowledge the joke. With the dog finally subdued and drinks to help them settle, Steve made another attempt to put his arm around his wife. He moved his arm slowly so as not to alarm Scratchy. For once, the dog seemed to not care if anyone petted her or not, and this time, Nancy didn't move away. From the kitchen came the smell of prepared food. Despite the tension, everything at least appeared normal.

"What did you do in Pennsylvania?" asked Nancy when the silence lingered.

Aunt Dolly chose that moment to pass through the room with oven mitts and a tray of food. Hearing the question, she stopped in her tracks. "Oh, come on, you can tell them now, Reuben."

Uncle Reuben studied his wife like a man suddenly faced with a question of life or death. Then his gaze shifted to Nancy. It looked as if he didn't know who he should kill.

"You said you worked on GPS," Nancy said.

"I did, didn't I?" he said like he'd almost forgotten. "But I never left Pennsylvania. Not physically, at least."

Nancy sat up straighter, forcing Steve to move his arm. "I imagine it was difficult being away from your family."

"Very difficult. I dreamed a great deal. All under close supervision. You see—" He paused, looking suddenly confused. "Didn't this happen already? All of us sitting here, me telling you this story?" Once more, he regarded Aunt Dolly and added, "Even though I shouldn't?"

Steve and Nancy shook their heads and waited for him to continue. Finally, he nodded to himself. "Maybe I've already seen this moment and I just can't remember. And if it's already happened, it's supposed to happen, and so I should get it over with and tell you the whole thing." He sighed. "I was involved in a special operation involving sleep. It's how GPS came about, you know. The whole thing happened by accident, as major developments often do. It started with a nap I took aboard a plane—and not just any plane, but the Concorde. You remember that funny looking bird, don't you? The ugliest plane ever built, but capable of speeds that went beyond Mach 2. Ugly, but fast as shit."

He went on to describe how a chance after-hours encounter with a Concorde pilot led to the flight. While out with a group of his intelligence coworkers, Reuben met the pilot in a DC bar. Several drinks later and everyone quite pickled, tongues started to loosen, and a few of the less discrete in their number began bragging about their respective security clearances. Eager to demonstrate his own clout, the pilot boasted that he could take them to Dulles Airport at that very moment and get them all on board the Concorde, which he would use to fly them around the world while still having them back in time for work the next day.

"The pilot said twelve hours," explained Uncle Reuben. "He could get us around the whole earth in *just twelve hours*. I already knew it was true, but I called bullshit anyway. I think I even called him a communist after watching him choke down his sixth or seventh Moscow Mule. Keep in mind that we had to be careful in those days. The Kremlin kept those DC bars full of KGB agents. But the pilot showed us his credentials, and he swore up and down he could get us on that plane and make it happen. So we said, 'Okay, Buck Rogers, put up or shut up.' Well, he did it, but not like we thought he would."

Uncle Reuben's cap already sat low on his forehead, but he pulled it even further as he sat up and leaned toward them.

"It turned out that we didn't *really* go around the earth. In reality, we used the earth's rotation. So the pilot flew north until we reached the North Pole. While over the polar region, he made a 180 degree turn and then flew south, all the way to Antarctica. Then he turned again, and flew all the way back to Dulles. Because his flight pattern worked with the rotation of the earth, we really did cover the whole globe—or I guess, technically, the earth rotated under us. Not that we paid attention. Things got a little wild in the lounge area of the plane with more drinking, even some mild public fornication amongst my more promiscuous colleagues. The whole plane smelled musky and sweaty, not at all like you'd expect on a high-tech aircraft. You all know what a naked body smells like, especially a woman's body, don't you?" He paused and waited for someone to answer. When no one did, he continued. "The whole plane was like that. One large body. No fornication for me, though." Here, he shot a glance back toward Aunt Dolly, but she no longer stood there, having taken the dinner tray on to the table in the dining room.

"At least none that I recall," Uncle Reuben said. "You see, someone, I think maybe the pilot himself, spiked my gin and tonic with some kind of psychotropic drug. I'd taken part in my fair share of psi-ops during that era, most of them utter failures. But this one was different. Something experimental. I think it was all planned, the whole thing, us meeting the pilot in that bar, him offering to get us all on that plane. In any case, I fell asleep almost immediately, thanks to the influence of this drug. It was the sleeping while traveling at such high speeds that did it—that *unlocked* something." Reuben paused here, his attention drawn to the television.

"What did it unlock?" Nancy asked the question in a

breathless tone.

No answer at first as Uncle Reuben returned his attention to the television. On the screen, a weather alert scrolled beneath images of dark clouds and waves battering a shoreline. It seemed at first as if he'd forgotten all about anyone else in the room. But then he spoke:

"It changed how my brain worked. How I saw things. My memory. I started remembering things that hadn't even happened yet."

"Like déjà vu?" asked Nancy.

"No, not like déjà vu. Much different." From outside came a great thunder that shook the walls. Then a sound came from high up in the rafters. The house shifting, most likely. Scratchy looked up at the ceiling and whined, but thankfully, she didn't bark. "Time stopped making sense," said Uncle Reuben. "It no longer seemed linear. Even physical space seemed to no longer matter. I could describe places I'd never been. I could picture them clearly. Someone could stand on a mountain in Switzerland and hold up a sign. Back in Pennsylvania, I would know exactly what the sign said. At the same time, my short-term memory went away. I couldn't remember what happened two hours ago, but somehow, I would know what would happen two hours later. Sometimes I couldn't see things happening right in front of me, but I could see things happening on the other side of the planet. It feels like I never got off that plane. I shouldn't be telling you all this."

"No, please," said Nancy. She leaned forward, positioning herself further away from Steve. "Go on."

Uncle Reuben regarded Nancy. He cocked his head and looked almost puzzled. "Did you bring a big blue and white cooler with you?"

"We did," said Steve. "But I'm sure we mentioned it to you."

Uncle Reuben ignored Steve and kept looking at Nancy. "You should get rid of it. Where is it right now?"

"In the back seat of our car," said Steve. "Tell us what that has to do with anything."

"They need a chance to go to the bathroom first." Everyone turned to see that Aunt Dolly had returned from the dining room. "Dinner's ready soon," she said.

"Didn't you just bring it out?" asked Steve.

Aunt Dolly looked down at her hands and saw that she wore oven mitts. "Oh. Is it on the table already? Did I already put it there?"

Uncle Reuben pointed at the drinks held by Steve and Nancy. "I think I'll have what they're having."

"You can't," Aunt Dolly said. "We take medicine." She looked questioningly at Stacey. "Don't we?"

Stacey slapped the armrest of the loveseat where he'd seated himself comfortably. "We'll take a break from the pharmaceuticals and all partake." No longer shirtless, he'd cooled off and had stopped perspiring. All that changed when he stood and began making his way toward the cache of old wine under the stairs.

"She's right," said Uncle Reuben, calling after him. "I can't, and neither should you. We all take medicine." But Stacey had already moved out of sight. "Anyway, that's how my work on GPS started. Asleep aboard a jet flying at twice the speed of sound, drugged out of my mind on God-knows-what, a guinea pig in someone's idea of a top-secret experiment. I guess it eventually paid off. GPS was a whole new thing back then."

"It must have been exciting," said Steve.

"It was horrible," Uncle Reuben said. "The lingering effects, I mean. I never knew quite where I was after that. And when I slept, it became much worse. That's why I went to Pennsylvania all the time—so I could sleep while they collected data on where I'd been."

"While you were asleep?" asked Steve. "I don't understand."

Uncle Reuben nodded slowly. "Did I ever tell you about the pickle jar?"

"Pickle jar?" Steve laughed and glanced around nervously, as if he might find the pickle jar on display somewhere in the room. "I don't think so."

Uncle Reuben covered his face with both hands and moaned. "Oh, Jesus, the pickle jar."

Then the rotating earth itself responded to his despair. The thunder cracked, and the lights flickered twice before the power went off in the house. Everything went dead, the only illumination coming from flashes of lightning. No one said a word. They listened to the sound of their own breathing, as well as more sounds coming from the rafters overhead. Once more, Scratchy whined. To their collective relief, the power returned quickly. When it did, they saw Aunt Dolly standing in the middle of the room, her head, like Scratchy's, turned up toward the ceiling.

"Dinner's served," she said, continuing to look toward the ceiling and the heavens beyond.

10

"Who the Hell Is Hank Aaron?"

It turned out that Aunt Dolly's chicken cacciatore consisted of frozen chicken tenders smothered in honey and ketchup, everything topped off with mozzarella cheese melted in the microwave. Steve stepped away to refill his glass and Nancy's while Nancy picked hesitantly at her food. Across from her sat Uncle Reuben, with Aunt Dolly seated next to him, across from Steve. Stacey took the chair at the head of the table. On the table sat the several bottles of wine he collected from the cache under the stairs, each one coated thick with dust.

"Where's that corkscrew?" asked Stacey. "We have one, don't we?"

"No, we don't," Uncle Reuben said in between bites of his meal. He seemed to enjoy the food a great deal. If nothing else, it seemed to alleviate all signs of the despair he felt just moments ago.

Buoyed by the second glass of brandy, Steve toasted the excellent cooking and the chef behind it. When no one joined him in raising a glass, he resumed the subject of the pickle jar. "I honestly don't recall you ever mentioning it."

Uncle Reuben wiped his mouth with a napkin and tugged down his cab driver's cap so that it nearly covered his eyes. "Are you sure I didn't already tell you about the pickle jar? I'd hate to tell that story again."

"Maybe I forgot."

"You wouldn't forget it." He used his fork to spear another delicious bite, but he didn't bring it to his lips. His face showed signs of a growing realization. "Or maybe I tell you tonight, and I'm just remembering something that hasn't happened yet. The memory and the event are just occurring out of sequence. Yes, that's probably the answer. That makes sense because we're not worried about security clearances anymore."

"I know we have a corkscrew somewhere," said Stacey. "Tell me where it is."

Either no one knew where to find a corkscrew or no one wanted to answer. Instead, they all watched in silence as Uncle Reuben rested his elbows on the table and folded his hands. "You remember that old house we had? The one near DC?"

"I have a story about that house," said Stacey. "Steven does too. Don't you, Steven?"

Uncle Reuben waved him off. "That house was built on ancient land. Sacred land. A creek ran behind it, and we enjoyed lots of privacy thanks to the acreage of woods surrounding it. Between the creek and the ridge sat two Indian burial mounds that I considered clearing out and leveling. Only I never did. Don't ask me why. Goddamned nuisance, they were."

"I remember those mounds very well," said Stacey. "I don't suppose Steven does. He always seemed focused on other things."

Nancy watched for Steve's reaction, but he didn't take the bait. "I remember a long driveway winding its way up a hill," said Steve, gesturing with his fork toward Uncle Reuben as if he'd remembered the most important detail in the world.

"Surely, you remember more than that," Stacey said.

Everyone ignored Stacey so Uncle Reuben could continue: "Once in a while, I'd put on my work clothes and putter about around the creek, occasionally clearing away debris. Sometimes I would visit the mounds. Occasionally, I'd find evidence of something digging around them—bears or raccoons or something else, I had no idea. I never saw a living creature around the mounds, so it was tempting to think something was digging its way out. The atmosphere of that place could cast quite a spell. So beautiful and strange. I spent most of my time under a canopy of trees so thick they nearly blocked out the sun. In that spot, the creek always seemed to run the fastest, and I'd like to stand there, imagining myself an early explorer, discovering God's green earth, free and untamed, just waiting for someone—for me—to shape it into something useful. Sometimes I'd take off all my clothes and let the water flow over me, wondering what it would feel like just to give myself to its currents and let them take me wherever they wanted to. I would find old arrow heads there occasionally. Even broken bits of pottery. It felt like a different world altogether."

Nancy smiled. "It sounds nice."

"It was. I liked to do this after my lengthy trips to Pennsylvania." He met the eyes of the two people across from him, daring them to challenge the veracity of a place called *Pennsylvania*. "During one particularly grueling trip, I slept for twenty hours straight. You'd never think that sleep could make someone exhausted, but it always did that to me. I know how strange it sounds, but sleeping for twenty hours night after night wears you out. Especially when it's your job. I used to piss like a racehorse afterwards. You'd have loved it." Here, he waved his fork at Aunt Dolly. She nodded and smiled. "Anyway, it seemed like the only way I could rest after such grueling sleep was by getting outside and doing physical work."

He paused for a bite of chicken. He chewed and peered inside himself, and they all watched, anxiously waiting to hear what he would say next. Even Stacey refrained from commentary.

"During one of those extended naps, I went somewhere. In fact, I traveled farther than I've ever traveled. In fact, I did so aboard a vessel of some sort. I don't know who built it or where it came from. Beings of some kind, maybe the ones responsible for everything I saw and experienced after the Concorde flight. I have no idea. These people are very blurry to me. Maybe they're not even people, at least not in the way we think of people. Very gray in complexion, not like you and me. Big melon-sized heads with black eyes and tiny mouths. Also, I'm not a tall man, as you know, but every one of them was shorter than me." He paused. "None of you believe me. You think I'm full of shit."

Aunt Dolly perked up at this remark. "Maybe you need to use the bathroom."

Uncle Reuben shook his head. "I'm holding it. I'd really like to finish this story. If you all want me to."

"I do," said Nancy. Her untouched food grew cold.

"Anyway," Uncle Reuben said, "they took me aboard their vessel, their craft. No one wore clothes, not even me. Honestly, it was very freeing. No one acted self-conscious or tried to cover themselves with anything. And here is the interesting part: none of the crew had genitals. No tiny little penis. No clefts or slits either. I still knew some of them were women.

Don't ask me how I knew that. The rest were men."

"As it should be," said Stacey. "There are only two genders, despite what the satanists and liberals try to tell you."

Nancy's jaw slackened as she started to say something, but Steve touched her wrist. "Go on, Uncle Reuben," Steve said, "we're listening."

Uncle Reuben nodded. "Everything on this craft was monochrome and sterile, like something in a space movie. Only we weren't exploring the cosmos, though the craft looked like it could do that. Instead, we traveled through *time*. One of the pilots came and sat with me for a while to explain why they'd taken me aboard. It—or *he*—told me how they used my brainwaves to not only map the topography of the earth but also its *past and present.* He said they planned to take me back to the year 1890 and land on the ridge overlooking my property so that I could see what it looked like decades before I would ever own it. And we did just that. They even brought along a picnic basket. I know it sounds like I'm making this shit up, but they had an honest-to-god wicker basket full of crackers and preserves in it, along with cheese and pickles. The craft landed on the ridge overlooking the creek and the Indian burial mounds, and we all disembarked, carrying this picnic basket like it was *The Sound of Fucking Music.* After walking a short distance, we all sat down and ate."

"Still naked?" asked Steve.

"Oh, yeah, but it didn't matter. None of us cared. Pretty soon, we finished all the food, and the beings who piloted the craft started packing everything back into the picnic basket. Then as we started heading back to where the craft waited on the crest of the ridge, I stopped and asked if I could have a minute alone, just to take in the view and reflect. They said of course.

In fact, they wanted me to reflect on the terrain and study it, like I was some kind of recording device, so they left me there all alone on that ridge. Whether they knew it or not, I don't know. I mean, I wore no clothes, so I had no place to hide it. Certainly not in my ass." He paused to dab at his mouth with a napkin. "But in any case, I held on to an empty pickle jar. Just to play a little trick."

He took a deep breath and studied his audience to make sure they paid attention. Even Stacey appeared anxious to hear what he would say next.

"I threw the pickle jar down toward the creek. I put all my strength into it, heaving it like Hank Aaron would gun one to third base, and I watched it soar over the trees and vanish. I couldn't see where it landed. I didn't know if I threw it far enough or if those beings saw me do it. Or even if they cared. Either way, I caught up with them, and we all went back inside the craft and returned home. Now, mind you, when I woke up in Pennsylvania, I had no memory of any of this, not the craft or the beings or the picnic. Until . . . until . . ." He held up his index finger and squeezed his eyes shut, trying to pull himself together.

"Until I went down to that creek one beautiful morning to clear away debris. There, under brambles and broken limbs, I found it. Right there, in the creek, half buried under silt. I didn't know what it was at first, so I dug it out, and right there, on the glass, I could still read the label. It said, *Guss' Pickles.* For all those decades, it lay there, right where it landed when I threw it, waiting for me to find it. I stood there in the creek, staring at that jar, and it all came back to me. Every moment. From that point on, I proved useless to the project, so they stopped sending me to Pennsylvania. Only I kept feeling the effects of those experiments. It's as though I've become responsible for all of history. Time has never been right for me since."

Uncle Reuben bowed his head as if in prayer. The ponderous weight of the silence fell over everything. Not even the thunder outside could disturb that silence. That silence drowned out everything.

Finally, Uncle Reuben lifted his head. His hand disappeared under the table, and like a magician conjuring a rabbit out of thin air, it returned holding a corkscrew. He passed it over to Stacey. "Here."

Stacey cheered as he opened one of the ancient bottles of wine and filled the empty tumbler in front of him to the brim with cloudy liquid full of floating sediment.

"I have just one question," Stacey said after enjoying his first sip. "Who the hell is Hank Aaron?"

"What's that?" asked Uncle Reuben. He took the bottle of wine from Stacey and poured himself a glass too. "Why are you asking me about Hank Aaron?"

"Because in your story, you mentioned him."

"Don't drink that," said Aunt Dolly to no one in particular, "or you'll be in the bathroom all night."

"I don't need to go anymore," Uncle Reuben said. He quickly gulped the wine and began scratching under his cap. Aunt Dolly shrugged and took some of the wine herself before offering the bottle to Steve and Nancy. They both took one look at the sediment floating in the wine and declined the offer.

"Hank Aaron is a famous baseball player," Nancy said. She paused before adding, "He started in the Nego Leagues. He was one of the greatest players who ever lived."

"I doubt that," said Stacey. "Honestly, how would you even know?"

"Nancy loves baseball," Steve said. "She's a huge Braves fan."

"And what I said is a fact," said Nancy quietly. "Everyone's heard of Hank Aaron."

They watched as Stacey took the bottle and emptied the rest of the wine into his tumbler. As he poured, he said, "You think you know a lot, Nancy, but I know something you don't know. In fact, I'll tell you all a story too. A story I know about *that* house. A story about Carla."

Steve grimaced. "No, please don't—"

"*She should know.* So you all be quiet. It's my turn to tell a story."

11

"I Never Went Into the Attic"

"It helps to know that I was never one of the cool kids, even when I was skinny. I guess there was something about me that kept me from clicking with others. From really connecting. Oh, but how I idolized my cousin. I practically worshipped him." Stacey winked in Steve's direction, a gesture that went unnoticed by Steve because he'd turned to look at Nancy, desperately trying to communicate without speaking. His hands fidgeted restlessly, unsure of what to do with themselves. Finally, he loaded another helping of chicken cacciatore onto his plate, even though he'd barely touched the first serving.

"I idolized my sister too," Stacey said, "especially since she knew how to make friends, not to mention how she enjoyed a much closer relationship with Steven than I ever would." He paused to consume the rest of his wine in one great gulp. Then he saluted Steve with his empty glass. "For as long as I could remember, I'd follow the both of you around, hoping you'd let me join the little games you'd play together. I guess it's understandable, since you were a couple of years older than me, but I still craved your attention more than anything. Sometimes you'd indulge me and say we were going to play hide-and-go-seek. Somehow in those games, I always wound up being 'it.' So I'd go off into a corner and count to fifty or whatever, and when I reached the end, I'd say in a loud, clear voice, *'Here I come!'* I always played fair and by the rules, you know. Then I'd go hunting for you in that great big house."

He paused to look at Uncle Reuben. "By the way, why did we have such a big house if you were always off in Pennsylvania? Why do we always have such big houses with so much space to hide in?"

Uncle Reuben didn't answer. He watched the sediment floating in his glass.

"Everyone likes to hide, I suppose. Anyway, I thought I knew all the good hiding places. I figured I would eventually get a turn to hide somewhere, and I knew the best place too. You know where?" He used a smile to try to tease them into guessing, but no one did. "Those Indian burial mounds. Oh yes, I would visit them when I felt alone. All the time, in other words. Scratchy liked to follow me down there, and she would play in the creek while I sat and meditated on the rocks. I wondered what was inside those mounds. I knew the Egyptians liked to hide treasure in their tombs, but what about Indians? Did they have gold or pearls or anything worth money? Once, Scratchy seemed to sense what I was thinking, because she went over to the base of one of the mounds and started whining, pawing at the packed mud and dirt. Before I could stop her, she found an area where she could burrow. She continued to dig with such excitement and desperation that I assumed she'd found the hiding place of a rabbit. Eventually, she cleared away enough room to squeeze half her body inside, and I watched her tail wag as she pushed deeper and deeper inside the mound. I couldn't wait to see what she found. 'Get it, Scratchy!' I said. 'Get it, get it!' She didn't need any encouragement from me. Eventually, her whines turned to growls as she fought something inside. But those sounds quickly changed back into whines and then yelps of pain. I watched helplessly as something dragged her all the way inside, leaving a big, empty hole at the base of that mound."

Stacey examined the faces around him. "Don't you all want to know what was inside? I sure wanted to know. I waited to see if anything would come out. I didn't even think about my own safety. I just wanted to see what had the strength to drag away a dog that big. Eventually, I found out, but not that day. You see, I stared so long into the darkness of that hole that the sun started going down, and the air grew chilly. Finally, I got scared and went back inside. But the next day, I returned, and guess what I found lying next to the creek, just outside the hole in that mound. Can you guess? Can you, Steven?"

He paused to allow a response from Steve, as if only his mattered. His mouth firmly set, Steve wouldn't give him the pleasure, so Stacey went on.

"I found Scratchy—or what was left of her. Something stripped all the flesh from her bones. It looked like something ate her up completely, all her fur, hide, and muscle, leaving just a skeleton behind. Nothing else, not even blood. Just bones. What could possibly do that? I *had* to know. I *had* to find out what was inside that mound. But I wasn't about to crawl inside it, *not on your life*. I had more sense than that. I left and brought back a flashlight, the strongest and brightest I could find, and I found the courage to get close enough to shine its light inside that hole. But I couldn't see anything. The blackness inside that hole was just too much for the light. Not giving up, I found a broken tree branch near the creek, and I used that to poke inside. But the tunnel went too far and too deep. Finally, I hollered as loud as I could into that hole, and I expected to hear an echo. But no. Instead, the hole swallowed up the sound of my voice, the same way it swallowed the light. Just as I started to give up, I heard an answer. Do you know what I heard? Do you know *who* I heard?"

No one would hazard a guess, so he told them.

"God. I heard the voice of *God*. *God* was alive inside of that mound. At first, I couldn't believe it. How could God possibly live inside something built by a tribe of heathens who didn't even believe in Him? I asked that question, making sure to keep my tone respectful, and He said, *Don't you know I am everywhere?* But still, an Indian burial mound seemed like an awfully strange place, only I didn't say it out loud. But I didn't need to. As God, he could read my thoughts. *Have faith, Stacey,* he said, *missionaries brought me here many, many years ago when they blessed this place.* That made sense, but why on earth did He do what He did to Scratchy? He said I'd given Him a blood sacrifice to prove my faith, and now, as a reward, He would bestow a blessing upon me. He asked me what I wanted more than anything in the world. Can you imagine God personally asking you that question? I could say anything—a million dollars, a girlfriend, a *million* girlfriends. But I wanted something so much simpler than that. You're all going to laugh at me when I tell you. I told Him how much I wanted Steven and Carla to include me in their games. In other words, to treat me like an equal. So don't laugh when I tell you that I asked God to tell me where I could find Carla and Steven when we played hide-and-go-seek."

No one laughed. Except Stacey.

"He told me where to look the next time we played. It was a place I never even thought to look. All those times I'd count to fifty and go through that great big dark house, looking for Carla and Steven, I would get frustrated and give up. I even tried turning it into a game I played with myself, pretending I was leading an expedition into the darkest corners of Africa, hunting gorillas and wild beasts, all while trying to avoid primitive spears and arrows of hostile tribesmen. I'd open each door, hoping to find my quarry; nothing. Only darkness would spill out. After a while, it got so tiring. Just once, Steven, I hoped you'd spend time with me alone. I wanted us to sit quietly and look at comics together, the way we used to when we were younger. In fact, I'm hoping we can do that together later. You can come back to my room, and—"

Aunt Dolly surprised everyone by speaking up.

"Oh, no, don't do that." Aunt Dolly's voice rose in pitch, and she shifted position, causing her wig to go askew, revealing part of her bald scalp. "You don't want to go in there!"

"Will you shut the fuck up?" Stacey slammed his fist on the table, causing one of the empty bottles to fall over and roll off the table. It managed not to break, but it landed near Scratchy, causing the dog to yelp. She quickly padded out of the room.

Aunt Dolly's outburst ended, but she didn't correct the position of her wig. She stared at Steve with an expression of terror.

Satisfied that the floor still belonged to him, Stacey resumed speaking. "I'll be honest with you, Steven. I envied you. I still do. To this day, I've never had a girlfriend—or at least one who didn't expect renumeration for the honor of me calling her that. One of them even taught me that word—*renumeration.* But as a youngster during that summer you visited, I just wanted you to love me as much as I loved you. If I could just show you that I wasn't some little kid you could hide from, I would finally win your affection. With my father off doing whatever he did in Pennsylvania and my mother off doing whatever she did, we had the whole house to ourselves. You, me, and Carla. So much space to hide in. If I could just find you, we'd stop playing that stupid game and you would spend time with me instead. Finally, thanks to the voice that spoke to me from the Indian mound, I knew where to look. *The attic.* Imagine that. I never thought to look there. So the next time I counted to fifty and went looking, I went straight there. Before I made it halfway up those wooden steps, I heard the sound of giggling that grew louder as I eased open the door. I heard something else too. Wet sounds. Kissing sounds. When I caught you in the corner with your arms wrapped around each other, I understood then why you always wanted to play that dumb kid's game."

Now Steve interrupted. He looked imploringly at his wife. "Nancy, I—" But he couldn't finish the sentence. He stopped as if she'd interrupted him, but she hadn't said a word. Her eyes watered and remained fixed on Stacey.

Stacey continued: "I knew then I would never measure up for you. I cried my eyes out. I even questioned my own faith. Why would God tell me to follow you into the attic knowing what a terrible discovery I'd make? What kind of *blessing* was that? I regretted going anywhere near that mound, thinking that maybe I'd found the devil instead of God. Only the devil would want to cause me the kind of hurt I felt. I'd already taken care of Scratchy's bones by storing them away safely in a box, but I decided I needed to do more than that. I needed to rid the land of that demon. So the next time I visited the mounds, I went with the idea of destroying them. I brought every tool I could find, shovels, pickaxes, anything available. But the work was too much for me. I needed a bulldozer. Besides, I kept hearing the voice. *Why are you doing this?* it said. *Why hast thou forsaken me?* I finally realized that I needed to do what Scratchy did—crawl inside and root the thing out with my bare hands. I didn't care what I saw it do to Scratchy. I didn't care about myself anymore. I didn't care about anything. So I crawled all the way inside, and I used the sound of its voice to tell which way to go until I finally found *it.* Its bones, at least. *God's bones,* I guess. *Why hast thou forsaken me?* it asked me again when I held the skull in my hand. Only God talks that way. It was proof. I cried to it, begging for help, asking what I should do. I sat on the edge of the creek, my body all scratched and filthy, holding God's skull in my hand, asking for guidance. When it spoke to me, it said, *Make an offering.* Only it wouldn't tell me what kind of offering to make. I thought and thought. What kind of offering could make me worthy of the love I wanted so much? Then it came to me."

"The party." Uncle Reuben spoke the words in a toneless whisper. He may as well have shouted it. Everyone turned to look at him.

"Yes," Stacey said, "a party! I'd host a party. That house with its size and remoteness made it the perfect party house. I would make it special by doing all the work myself as a special gift to Carla and Steven. An *offering* to them on a week when we had the house all to ourselves. What better gift than the biggest party anyone had ever seen. But how could I possibly find enough people to show up for a big party? I'll tell you how—by printing fliers and taking them everywhere, advertising the biggest party in the county! I even came up with the idea of making some money in the process by charging a small fee to everyone who attended. So I used colored markers and wrote out all the details, including the address. I made the directions quite detailed. No one had GPS in those days. Then, one day, we all went to movies, and you and Carla made me drive so you could snuggle in the backseat together. I pretended I didn't want to see the movie you picked out. *Dirty Dancing*, I think. Steven, was that the movie?"

Steve shrugged, either not knowing or not caring, a gesture indicating he only wanted the story to end.

Stacey said, "I told you I wanted to see the new killer shark movie that just came out. But what I really did was wait for you and Carla to disappear into the theater. Then I left, taking my flier to the copy store, where I made two hundred copies. Once I had those in hand, I drove around town, handing them out at basketball courts, diners, everywhere I could. I managed to get every one of those copies into circulation before it was time to meet the two of you at the movie theater. I had an answer ready in case you asked me how I liked the *Jaws* movie, but neither of you cared enough to ask. Still, as I drove us home, I felt proud of myself. I imagined that for every flier I gave out, at least one person would show up for the party later that week. If I collected five dollars from each one of those people, I'd make a thousand dollars."

Stacey's face beamed with pride, but no one congratulated him on his early attempt at entrepreneurship. Aunt Dolly's expression remained frozen in horror, while Uncle Reuben gazed blankly at his wine glass.

"Well, the day of the party came, and I couldn't keep it a secret any longer. When I finally told Steven and Carla, imagine the misery I felt when they told me how stupid I was. 'But Stacey, we don't have any food or drinks.'" Here, Stacey's voice rose, becoming shrill and high-pitched. "And that was true. I hadn't thought of that. So we all went out that day and used Steven's fake ID to buy lots of beer and wine. Like this one."

He picked up an untapped wine bottle and emptied it into his cup. They watched as he drank most of it in one gulp and wiped his mouth.

"It turned out that it didn't matter. People brought lots of things with them. Not just alcohol but drugs too. Later, the police estimated that over eight hundred people showed up."

His face still impassive, Uncle Reuben interrupted. "Eight hundred and fifty," he said.

"Was that the number?" asked Stacey. "It's impressive how numbers don't leak out of your brain with practically everything else, so I have to assume you're right. That means I should have made . . ." He stopped to do the math.

"Four thousand, two hundred fifty," Uncle Reuben said.

"I'll trust you on that," said Stacey, "but I managed to only pocket three hundred. I couldn't keep track of who showed up at the house. It was simply too overwhelming. People came through every entrance, even the windows. They filled every room. Part of the house even caught on fire. When the helicopter showed up, they even saw people on the roof, waving to them. Apparently, they climbed out a window to escape the smoke. Other areas of the house managed to avoid both fire and smoke."

"The damage was immense," said Uncle Reuben.

Stacey ignored him. "People even piled into bathtubs, naked and passed out on top of each other. Furniture soiled and destroyed. People even went into the attic. Right, Steven?"

Steve nodded and looked down at his plate. "Right," he said

softly.

"Because that's where I found Carla. Once I found out about the fire, I went looking for you, and I thought for sure I'd find you both in there. Only I couldn't stay in there long. The smoke made it hard to see anything, not to mention breathe. I would have left right away, but I thought I heard you calling out for me. *Help me, Stacey, help me.* I staggered around, thinking I'd find the two of you huddled together, waiting for me to rescue you. But no. I only found Carla. If not for the condition of her body—the mess—someone might have thought she was sleeping, though who could sleep naked on the bare floor? All around her, I saw the bones I'd taken out of the Indian mound, everything scattered around, even the skull, its dead eyes staring at me. The box I kept them in lay tilted over in the corner, like someone went rummaging around in it. I concluded it had to be you who did it, Steven. Only with the smoke burning my eyes, I couldn't see where you were hiding, even though it could only have been *your* voice I heard. But I didn't have time to play another game of hide-and-seek. So I covered up Carla. I didn't want the police to find her like that. I also didn't want them to find the bones I'd collected, so I moved those to a safe place where only I would know where to find them. I had enough wits about me to know that the police wouldn't leave human remains behind. They'd have a lot to say about that, just like they had a lot to say about how I shouldn't have touched Carla's body."

Nancy wouldn't look at Steve. Unblinking, she stared at Stacey. Through the windows came a flash of lightning so intense that it turned the room white. Everyone jumped except Nancy, who went on staring, waiting for the story to continue.

"They say I contaminated evidence, whatever that means,"

Stacey said. "But how much evidence does anyone need to see that she passed out and choked on her own vomit? Someone tried saying it was me who took off her clothes, but why would I do that? To my own sister? Especially with the smoke in the attic? It's a good thing the fire never spread very far. You didn't see any fire in the attic when you were in there, did you, Steven? You didn't leave her up there when the smoke started coming in?"

Steve cleared his throat. He lifted his head and said, "I never went into the attic. Ever."

"Oh," Stacey said, "I guess I'm remembering things all wrong. I suppose you did say that very thing to the police. *'I never went into the attic.'*"

"It's true. I didn't." Steve touched Nancy's hand and repeated it. "It's true." But Nancy pulled away her hand.

"You helped a lot in the clean-up," said Stacey. "I remember you staying with us for another week just to do that. Everyone was very grateful."

"Everyone?"

All eyes turned to Uncle Reuben to see what he would say next.

"Everyone?"

He appeared stuck on that word. He said it two more times before finally adding, "I think dinner is over. I think—" His face contorted, and with an index finger, he reached under his cab driver's cap as if he suddenly experienced a stinging itch somewhere on his scalp. At the same time, thunder shook the walls. Scratchy, who'd quietly re-entered the room at some point, erupted in a fit of barking.

No one reached down to pet Scratchy, so the barking only intensified, and Uncle Reuben's grimace grew worse as he continued digging under his cap with his finger. Finally, he stopped and looked down to where Scratchy sat beneath the table. *"Will you please shut up, please, shut up, shut it, shut up the shit?"*

No one paid attention to the dog any longer. Nor did Uncle Reuben's increasingly incoherent outburst matter to them.

Because he'd begun to bleed. From beneath his cap, streams of blood ran down his temples, across his cheeks, and down to his lips. Still, he seemed to not notice, and he continued yelling at the dog.

"Fucking fuck dog, shit it up, up, up, shit."

The blood continued to flow and now painted his entire face. He looked and sounded like a demon, like something that escaped the prison of an ancient grave.

"I think we should all use the bathroom," said Aunt Dolly. She grabbed a clean napkin and began dabbing ineffectually at her husband's face.

"Oh my god," said Nancy, "you're bleeding too."

Aunt Dolly stopped her dabbing and looked at Nancy's accusing finger, her expression puzzled, apparently not realizing that blood had begun seeping down from beneath her wig. Uncle Reuben continued to berate the barking dog, his words reduced to meaningless blather. No one could understand him at all. During the chaos, his hat became dislodged, revealing a bald head with mottled age spots and what looked like a series of round holes, each one roughly the size of a bullet, the source of the bleeding. Aunt Dolly struggled to help him, finally managing to get the hat properly reseated on his head. Only then did she finally understand why Nancy continued to point at her. She felt the blood on her cheek and reached up to adjust her wig.

"*I* need to use the bathroom," she said.

12

"Except in English"

No one cleaned up after dinner, the plates with their scraps of food left to go to waste on the table. The unexpected display of blood left Steve and Nancy unnerved and in a state of disbelief. Stacey offered them answers after he returned from helping his parents clean themselves up and reset their respective head pieces. "They both had surgery recently," he said. "Brain tumors. They'll probably die at the same time, eventually. For now, they're both resting comfortably. As a member of the family, you deserve to know."

He spoke these words to Steve, even though Nancy stood in the vicinity. Since dinner, she'd maintained a good deal of distance between herself and Steve. Outside, the wind and rain showed no signs of abating, and thunder occasionally shook the walls.

"I got a good look at those holes in his head," said Nancy. "It looked like someone made them with a drill."

Stacey suffered a glance in her direction. "I assure you, they were made by a professional. They benefited from the best surgical equipment."

"I want to make sure they're okay," she said.

"They're obviously *not* okay, Nancy. Did you hear what I said? They have brain cancer. Besides, my mother doesn't want anyone in her bedroom. She barely tolerates me back there."

Nancy made a frustrated sound, but before she could put her defiance into action, Scratchy began barking again, announcing that Uncle Reuben and Aunt Dolly had reappeared, their faces now mostly clean and some semblance of order restored.

"It's time for everyone to go to bed," Aunt Dolly said.

"I think I'm going to leave," said Nancy.

No one except Steve showed any reaction to her saying *I* instead of *we*. His mouth gaped in despair.

"No one is leaving," said Uncle Reuben. "The storm is worse. It's really coming down. You try to drive out now and you'll be stuck in water until the morning. People drown when it floods. It gets worse every year. I hear the land is sinking."

Outside, the thunder spoke its agreement.

"Make sure you use the bathroom before you go to bed," said Aunt Dolly. She gestured for them to follow as she started for the Jungle Room.

Nancy breathed rapidly as she followed Steve. Behind her walked Uncle Reuben, and Stacey lumbered at the rear, using furniture to keep himself balanced, the wine having disrupted his equilibrium. By the time the others climbed the stairs to the split level, he still clung to the railing, using it to pull himself up one step at a time.

Inside the enormous Jungle Room, they once more came face to face with the posed dog skeletons. Scratchy remained downstairs this time, content to stay away from this room.

"Do the sofas pull out?" asked Steve.

Aunt Dolly regarded him blankly. "Pull out of what?"

"This is fine," said Nancy. She set her handbag on one of the couches, thereby designating the other one for Steve. A thin curtain covered an enormous window, but it did little to diminish the effect of the lightning. Each flash seemed to punch a hole in time and space by proliferating the room with shadows, doubling the number of occupants in the room, including the dog skeletons. Rain thrashed the windowpane, trying to push its way in to drown them.

"The shower works," Uncle Reuben said. Near one of the dog skeletons, a half wall led to a small bathroom area.

"Good. I can use it," said Nancy. She looked at their hosts expectantly, meaning for them to leave.

"A shower during a storm is dangerous," Aunt Dolly said. "The lightning will get you."

"I'll be fine."

"It happens. If it doesn't kill you, it'll render you senseless. You'll shit the bed for the rest of your life."

"Sixty-six percent of household accidents occur in the bathroom," said Uncle Reuben.

"I'll be fine."

Aunt Dolly nodded. As she turned with her husband to walk out of the room, Stacey appeared in the doorway, nearly breathless from his climb up the stairs.

"Steven," said Stacey, "you promised me you'd come to my room."

Steve started to protest, but Nancy interrupted. "Just go."

"But we're going to shower."

"I'm going to shower. You go." She spoke without any discernable tone. An unvoiced accusation lingered in the air, punctuated by the sound of thunder.

Uncle Reuben and Aunt Dolly slunk out of the room during this exchange, leaving Stacey standing alone in the doorway. "Come along, then," Stacey said.

Steve lingered, but Nancy indicated that she considered him gone by busying herself with what she needed for her shower.

"Come on," said Stacey, a command now evident in his voice.

So, leaving Nancy behind, Steve followed Stacey to the landing, where the stairs extended to the next level of the house. There, the door leading to Stacey's room awaited them. His face set with determination, Stacey grasped the railing and resumed climbing, each step eliciting a grunt of displeasure. Steve followed reluctantly. Each step required great strength and stamina from Stacey, as well as patience from Steve, especially when, at the halfway point, they paused to rest.

"You'd think," Stacey said between gasps, "that with all this stair climbing, I'd lose some weight."

Steve said nothing.

"Do you think I will? Eventually?" asked Stacey.

"Sure," Steve said. "You're getting lots of exercise."

Instead of resuming the ascent, Stacey pointed toward their destination. "As the land sinks, that'll be the safest room in the house. And maybe I won't have to climb stairs anymore. That's why I chose it. Plus, it has a way into the attic."

Neither spoke further once the trek upwards commenced again. When they finally arrived, Stacey grasped the doorknob with an elated expression. "Are you ready?" he asked, and before Steve could answer, he swung the door open.

Only it didn't swing very far. Something butted up against it from the other side, requiring Stacy to squeeze through a narrow opening. Steve followed, and his eyes widened at the sight that awaited him: hundreds of boxes in stacks that nearly reached the ceiling. Each box looked much like what Steve helped deliver to the thrift shop earlier. The stacks even formed a similar kind of pathway through the large bedroom.

Stacey continued to lead as Steve followed. Because of their perilous, haphazard arrangement, the boxes looked dangerously close to falling and injuring someone. With his attention focused on them, Steve nearly tripped over a cordless drill left carelessly on the floor, its edges coated with an oily substance that glistened wetly in the dull light. "Keep going," Stacey said, and Steve obeyed, until they finally arrived at an unmade bed covered with sheets in bad need of laundering. Stacey took a seat on the mattress and indicated that Steve should sit down next to him.

This time, Steve didn't comply. "Look, that stuff you talked about earlier—I have such a bad memory of everything that happened. I know that was a bad week. Not just that, the worst. But it was so long ago. It's all so hazy to me."

Stacey smiled. "It's all in the past, Steven. You don't think I'd hold that against you, do you? I love you. Please, sit down. Next to me."

Steve remained standing. "I can hardly picture that old place anymore. Was there really an Indian burial mound? And you talk about an attic. I don't recall going into anyone's attic. I barely go into my own attic."

"Well, you'll be interested in knowing that this house was built to closely match that old home. Its structure, its dimensions, even its exterior paint. Practically the same. And that includes the attic. A person could live quite comfortably in that attic, believe it or not. There's an access point right over there." He pointed, but Steve couldn't see anything but wild stacks of boxes. "Please," Stacey said, "will you kindly sit down already?"

Steve made a sound of protest, but he did what Stacey wanted. With his added weight, the bed sagged and made an audible groan.

"Now, I've been saving these for a moment like this one." From the other side of the bed, Stacey gathered a stack of comic books with yellowing pages and tattered covers. "These come through the thrift store quite often, and they're amazing." He placed the stack onto Steve's lap. "I've saved you all the Gold Key titles. Notice the *Doctor Spektor* and the *Grimm's Ghost Stories*. I wish all of them had their covers, but beggars can't be choosers. Just look at the art work in those. There are others, of course."

Steve did a poor job of feigning interest as he sifted through the stack. Most of the comics consisted of faded remnants of past glory. Yet Steve paused at one of them, and Stacey leaned forward to see what caught his eye.

"Ah. *UFO Flying Saucers*. That's a good one. A rare title."

The cover depicted a gray-skinned alien with a bulbous head standing on a ridge, pointing down ominously at a hapless young man who gazed up in horror at a circular space craft. Steve opened the comic and surveyed the panels, which told the story of a man who commandeered the technology of an alien race so that he could go back in time to save his wife from dying of a rare disease. Someone had vandalized the comic, however, tearing out the last pages and thus leaving the ending of the story a mystery.

"The most interesting one is on the bottom, though," Stacey said. "I'd really like you to see that one." When Steve failed to respond, Stacey took the stack away from him and rifled through it until he found the comic he wanted.

Steve remained motionless as Stacey set the special artifact onto his lap.

"It's in Spanish, I think," said Stacey.

The cover of this comic looked more garish than the others, its artwork notably cruder and more adult in nature. It featured a bearded man wearing a black hat and a black cape, using a cane to beat a naked woman.

"I've never seen anything like this one, but I knew I had to have it," Stacey said. "I suppose that Nancy of yours could translate it, but I don't think it's appropriate for the eyes of the gentler sex. Do you?"

The heat emanating from Stacey's body made the whole room feel damp and wet. Steve tried to return the comic, but Stacey pushed it back. "Go on, open it. I can share." When it continued to sit unopened on Steve's lap, Stacey reached over and began turning the pages for him. Before their eyes passed more provocative scenes, all in explicit black and white. Stacey paused at one point so that Steve could take in the depiction of a wild-eyed man dragging the body of naked and presumably dead woman to a graveyard. No one needed to translate the captions to understand what he intended to do. After dumping the body into an open grave, he laughed maniacally as he unloaded a bag of lime on top of it. The next panel showed him refilling the grave with dirt before returning home to his castle, where he enjoyed a beautiful meal. Meanwhile, the hand of his victim, now stripped of flesh thanks to the lime, pushed its way through the grave dirt. In the final panels, the man in the castle went to his bedchambers, fully sated from his meal, only to have a skeleton with bits of undissolved flesh still clinging to its bones burst in upon him. The story's final panel showed the man screaming as the skeleton's hands began tearing him apart.

"I've been saving this one for a long time," said Stacey in a near breathless voice. "I find it fascinating."

Steve closed the comic and handed it over. "It's really interesting. Sure." He then produced a yawn. "I'm afraid it's been a long day. I should turn in."

Stacey nodded. "I suppose you don't want to leave Nancy alone. I'll bet you could never imagine your life without her."

"If she dies first," Stacey said, "what would you do? Would you live alone?"

The corners of Steve's mouth dropped. He stopped moving and remained on the bed. "Why would you ask me that?"

"Because I would want you to know that you don't have to live alone. You can come and live here. If you want. I always felt like you belonged here."

Steve's jaw went slack. He tried to stand, but the drooping mattress made it difficult. He looked like a man doomed by gravity.

Stacey said, "I remember you before you ever met Nancy. I'd bet that you would be doing more than writing technical manuals if you didn't have her. I'd bet you'd be writing things like this." He held up the comic. "Except in English."

"I think I'm pretty happy doing what I'm doing." Steve smiled with visible effort. "I'm happy with Nancy."

"If only you could go back in time just to make sure. Change a few things here and there."

"I'm leaving now. Goodnight, Stacey."

"Sure, Steven. Go ahead."

As Steve stood, he grunted and touched his ribs.

"You're not still hurting, are you?" asked Stacey.

Steve shook his head, but his hand lingered at his side.

"I saw how Leslie handled you. He treated you like a delicate butterfly. You should see what that man can do. If you need another adjustment, I can call him now, and he'll be right over."

"I'm fine. I need to get back to Nancy."

As Steve started down one of the pathways formed by the stacks of boxes, Stacey called him back. "Not that way," said Stacey, "unless you want to see the attic."

Steve shook his head and reversed course, using the correct pathway now. Periodically, he turned to look over his shoulder. The way behind him remained clear. The boxes that threatened to topple miraculously remained perched on top of one another. Once again, he passed the drill leaking the oily substance. The sight of it made him pick up his pace. Finally, he found the door to the bedroom. At first, it wouldn't open, but he jiggled the knob, and it finally gave. He stepped quickly into the hallway, where he paused briefly to listen to the wild noises of the rain and thunder before eventually descending the stairs to the chamber called the Jungle Room.

13

"I Haven't Changed"

Darkness welcomed him inside, and he spoke to it. "Nancy?"

No answer. Just the continuous sound of rain beating against the window.

A burst of lightning briefly illuminated the room, granting a momentary glimpse of what looked like Nancy's form under a blanket. She lay upon the couch furthest from the door. The dog skeletons seemed to retain the light once the darkness resumed and appeared to glow somehow. The other couch, the one closest to the door, waited for him.

First, he went into the bathroom and shut the door behind him. He found a light switch and saw a single damp towel on a hanger. On the sink sat a medicine bottle containing Nancy's sleep aid, an indication she took something to help her doze off.

He needed to pee, and when he lifted the toilet seat, he saw that Nancy used it before him. He tried flushing the toilet, but nothing happened when he used the lever.

It took him a few moments to figure out that the toilet had no apparent connection to water or possibly even a sewer line. It looked as if someone set it up for simulation and not for actual function.

He used it anyway. Then he tried the sink, letting out a relieved sound when it provided water. He picked up the sleep aid but set it back down without taking one. He splashed water on his face. As he used Nancy's towel to pat himself dry, something distracted him. A sound, perhaps just the house settling. Looking up, he noticed a hatch high up in the ceiling, no doubt the access point to the attic that Stacey referred to. He regarded it warily before turning off the light and returning to the Jungle Room.

"Nancy?" he said in a soft voice. "If you're awake, will you let me know?"

He waited for a reply, but the form on the couch failed to even stir. "I wish you would talk to me now. I saw something I'm trying to make sense of. And I know you heard some things tonight that have made you question me. I'm sure you want explanations. I want to tell you my side of things, only there's really not much to tell. I simply don't recall a lot of the things Stacey talked about. It was so long ago." He sighed. "I think we can at least agree that Stacey is a very disturbed individual, and it's possible he could be doing something we need to report to the proper authorities." His voice started to crack. "I just want to assure you I'm the same man you married. I haven't changed. I love you so much."

He stood still, but again, no reply and no sign of movement on the other couch. Finally, he moved through the darkness toward the vacant couch, stumbling several times before he actually found it. He began removing his clothes, barely making it down to his underwear before exhaustion overtook him. In moments, he began to snore.

14

"Esta Es Una Casa de Locos"

An unfamiliar sound awoke Nancy from a dream. In this dream, she lay naked upon a kind of slab, looking up into a clear blue sky. The slab's surface felt uneven on her back, like the coarse fingers of a giant prodding her rudely. A large rock, perhaps? She attempted to shift to a more comfortable position but found it impossible to move, her body in a state of paralysis. She tried to soothe herself by focusing on that beautiful sky, but then the faces appeared, featureless and blank, with blank, expressionless eyes, their skin the color of a reptile denied sunlight. No, more like that of a shark. Their small mouths betrayed no emotion as they all looked down upon her, five of them in all.

Her lungs refused to supply the air she needed to scream. She gulped like a fish flopping on the shore as the faces continued to regard her impassively. If only she could find something heavy within reach, something she could use as a weapon (her mind said: *pickle jar*) but her arms ignored her commands.

Then her arms opened, and she found herself in that terrible room again, her limbs too heavy to move. The sleep aid failed to keep her asleep, instead leaving her lethargic and immobile, just as she was in the dream.

Something moved in the room.

Flickers of light penetrated the darkness, creating the illusion that the dog skeletons shifted their positions, stalking her, moving in on her with the intention of ripping out her throat while she struggled out of her paralysis.

More sounds. Someone crawling, perhaps?

"Steve?" Her voice sounded tired and haggard. "Did you fall off the couch?"

No answer.

"Steve?"

After waiting several seconds, she tried it a different way.

"Steven?"

The name hung in the air, no longer a plea but an accusation. Still no answer. Just more sounds of movement, only closer now. Her eyes began to adjust to the darkness, even if the control of her muscles lagged. Across the room, where two skeletons sat hunched in the gloom, she saw what looked like Steve's body in deep slumber, his back facing her.

Then a pungent odor reached her, along with the echo of something heavy being dragged across the floor.

"Stacey?" she said, her voice barely a whisper.

Then a hand appeared, clasping itself over her lips, and she found herself choking on dust and dirt. The hand belonged to some wild thing, its face half-concealed by lanky hair that dripped with sweat. The sweat dripped on her face, the salt stinging her eyes. One bulging eye peered through the hair, wide with hate and desperation. It crawled on top of her, positioning itself on top of her chest like an incubus, its hand muffling the scream she tried to produce.

Only when it spoke did it become possible to think of *it* as *him.* A *person.* A naked human being.

"Mantén la boca cerrada o te mato*!*"

The voice cracked from disuse or dehydration or possibly both. It still rose above her feeble efforts to scream, still muffled by the fingers sealing her lips. The assailant used his other hand to squeeze her throat. His thighs pinned her arms against her side, rendering them completely useless.

"Deja de pelear conmigo. Entender?"

She nodded, but he maintained his hold over her.

"Esta es una casa de locos. Estay encondenado en el atico pero ahora estoy escapanado."

When he finished, he searched Nancy's face for understanding. Beneath his weight, Nancy struggled to worm her hand into the pocket of the pants she wore that day. The pants she decided to sleep in.

"*Bruja!* Crees que puedes apuñalarme?"

Using both hands now, he tightened his grip on her throat. She thrashed underneath him, her hand struggling to maintain hold of the small cross that she withdrew from her pocket, the one given to her earlier. Without air, her attempt at speech faltered. The man on top of her grunted as he squeezed even harder, his strength considerable despite his emaciated state. He could not have heard what she tried to enunciate, even if it were his own name.

15

"Maybe Dead"

A looming presence caused Steve to awaken with a start. How had he not heard Stacey come into the room and stand over him like that? His cousin's face glistened with perspiration, no doubt from the exertion it took him to come down the stairs. The fact that he accomplished this task so quietly seemed like an extraordinary feat.

"Steven? Thank the lord you're awake. Something awful has happened."

Steve clutched his chest. For once, no sounds of thunder and rain from outside. The sound of his galloping heart filled the quiet.

"Nancy. Where is she?" Steve sat up and looked about the room. A purple light fell over everything, its source unclear, but it made it difficult to distinguish shadow from form and thus difficult to discern the empty couch where Nancy once slept. A thin band of light came from under the bathroom door, and Steve watched it expectantly.

"She's not in there," said Stacey.

As if on cue, the bathroom door opened, and a massive form

blocked all the light from escaping. The person standing there zipped up the fly of their pants and turned off the light before stepping into the room. Now, the looming figure stood behind Stacey.

It was Leslie.

"Where's Nancy?" asked Steve. Perched on the edge of the couch with slumped shoulders, he looked like a pathetic spectacle in the presence of the two other men. He appeared beaten and confused.

"She's left. I'm so sorry, Steve. But she left you a note. Leslie?"

As if asked a question he anticipated, he walked over to the desk that held an old manual typewriter. He returned with a white piece of paper that he handed over to Stacey. Stacey passed it to Steve, who squinted as he struggled to read it in the purple light.

"She tried to wake you up, apparently. You must've been dead to the world. Once the rain finally stopped, she decided to take her chances and go. All her things are gone."

Steve made no reply. He stared at the typed, all-caps message.

DEAR STEVEN I AM SORRY BUT I CANT SLEEP AND NOW THE RAIN HAS STOPPED SO I AM GOING TO TRY MY VERY BEST TO GET HOME. I KNOW YOUR COUSIN STACEY WILL TAKE GOOD CARE OF YOU. HE GAVE ME VERY VERY GOOD DIRECTIONS TO FIND MY WAY BACK AND I WILL TRY NOT TO GO THE WRONG WAY. I WILL SEE YOU VERY SOON. LOVE NANCY

Once Steve finished reading, he turned the letter over and stared at the blank side for several seconds. Meanwhile, Leslie grew bored and began shadowboxing. Stacey watched his cousin's reaction carefully. "But that's not the terrible thing that happened. I haven't told you what that is yet."

Steve acted as if he hadn't heard Stacey. He didn't even look at him. Instead, he found where he'd thrown his pants onto the floor and rooted around in the pockets. After trying the first pocket, he moved on to the second, both times coming up empty. He moaned in frustration.

Stacey said, "I promise I'm telling the truth. You believe me, don't you?"

Leslie stopped shadowboxing and watched Steve quietly.

Still not answering, Steve picked up his phone and pressed the call dial. With the phone pressed to his ear, he stood and walked aimlessly around the room. Leslie and Stacey watched every move he made. Finally, Steve held the phone away from his ear and tilted his head, as if trying to hear the song of some rare species of bird.

"I bet it's going to voicemail," Stacey said. "She probably doesn't want to answer the phone because she's driving. And I gave her such good directions that she doesn't need her GPS."

When Stacey said *GPS*, Steve reacted as if he just thought of something. He pressed more buttons on his phone and stared at the screen. His brow furrowed. "She's stopped sharing her location with me."

Helplessly, he finally looked at Stacey and Leslie.

"She seemed pretty upset," said Stacey. "I didn't want to tell you that. She said she just needed to be alone to think about things."

Steve returned to his seat on the couch. He leaned forward with his elbows on his knees, his expression one of worry and despair. Leslie began shadowboxing again.

"I'm so sorry about Nancy," Stacey said, "but I haven't even told you about the terrible thing that happened."

"What could be more terrible," Steve said in a slow voice,

"than my wife taking my car and leaving me?"

"I can't say I know what that feels like," said Stacey with an embarrassed laugh. "I've never had a girlfriend. At least not officially. Leslie here has had lots of women. Hundreds. Maybe thousands."

Leslie stopped shadowboxing to make a crude thrusting gesture with his pelvis. That made Stacey laugh. Leslie maintained a straight face as he went back to shadowboxing.

Stacey cleared his throat and became serious again. "We've had a death in the house."

"What?" Steve squinted up at his cousin.

"Oh, don't worry. It's not my mother or my father. They're still sleeping. It's Scratchy."

"Scratchy?" Steve spoke the name as if he couldn't think of anyone called *Scratchy*.

"Scratchy. Yes. The dog." Stacey's eyes turned down, and he folded his hands in a gesture of mourning.

"Scratchy was fine last night. Tonight, I mean. Christ, what time is it?"

"The sun will be up soon," Stacey said. "And it doesn't matter how Scratchy was before. Those types of dogs don't live long. They never do. Five, six years tops. They can drop dead as young as four."

"I don't think that's right."

"I assure you it is. Look around you. As evidenced by what you see in this room, I clearly should know what I'm talking about."

With his elbows still resting on his knees. Steve buried his face in his hands. Stacey watched as his cousin tried to collect himself. Leslie stopped shadowboxing and watched too.

Finally, Steve dropped his arms and looked up at them. "I'm

sorry. You're right. I don't know. I don't own a Tibetan Mastiff. I don't own any sort of dog."

"They're very delicate animals. All the barking does is weaken their hearts, and as you saw, Scratchy loved to bark."

"Right. Look, I'm upset. My wife has gone, and I don't know what to do."

"We do." Stacey looked over at Leslie, who had grown bored again and resumed his shadowboxing. "You can help us carry the dog's body downstairs.

"I don't know. Nancy . . ."

". . . might come back. The activity will give you something to do."

Steve nodded and stood. He put on his clothes as Stacey and Leslie watched with intense focus. As he finished buttoning, Steve paused. Something on the floor caught his attention. The room's other occupants observed as Steve reached down for something that lay near his feet. He held the object and used the light of his phone to study it. "That's weird," said Steve.

Stacey and Leslie both moved closer to see what Steve held.

A tiny gold cross.

"That looks like an earring," Stacey said. "My mother is always losing hers."

"No," said Steve. He scratched his temple thoughtfully as he stared at the object. "I think it's—well, I don't know. Never mind." Quickly, he slid it into the pocket of his jeans. "I'll help you. Just let me wash up first."

But as Steve started for the bathroom, Leslie blocked his way. Steve looked at Stacey with questioning eyes.

"Nothing's working," Stacey said. "The storm has caused the sewers to back up. If you flush the toilet, the whole house might flood."

Steve looked like he had something to say, only he didn't know quite how to word it.

"The rain's stopped. You can use the trees outside. But first, help us with Scratchy." Stacey pointed toward the room's entrance, where something large lay on the floor covered by a blanket. Steve scrutinized it, his brow furrowing.

"That's Scratchy?"

"Yes."

"Why is Scratchy in this room?"

"This is where she died, Steven. She just fell over and expired like I told you."

"No, that can't be right." Steve's eyes roamed back and forth between Leslie and Stacey. "Scratchy didn't like to come in here. I saw for myself that she avoided this room like the plague."

Stacey laughed. "That's quite wrong. Scratchy loved this room. She liked to visit her friends."

"No, no," Steve said. He stared at the blanket on the floor and the lump beneath it. His eyes measured its dimensions, its mass.

"Steven? Do you want to see Scratchy before we take her downstairs? Maybe just to say goodbye?"

Steve's face turned back toward Stacey and Leslie, now assessing their dimensions, their mass. Finally, he spoke. "Yeah, I would. I really would."

Leslie made an irritated noise and made a move toward Steve, who shut his eyes in preparation for something that never came. Instead, Leslie gripped the edge of the blanket and flipped it back, revealing the dog's massive forepaw but not much more. He looked expectantly at Steve, waiting for the signal that he'd seen enough, which Steve provided by nodding. Leslie grunted and returned the blanket's edge to its former position, as if protecting the animal's modesty.

"Now that your curiosity's been satisfied," Stacey said, "will you help Leslie carry the dog downstairs? In my condition, I'm afraid, the effort would tax me severely. My knees aren't what they used to be."

Steve sighed and nodded. Keeping the dog decently covered with the blanket, he lifted one end of the dead animal while Leslie lifted the other. As he'd done so often recently, Stacey led a procession to the stairs, this one carrying a dread burden downward. Steve's position forced him to walk backwards, causing him to struggle to maintain his balance and hold on to the dog at the same time.

The dog's size made the labor demanding. "How did you know Scratchy died?" Steve managed to ask on the trek down the stairs.

Stacey didn't answer, so Steve repeated the question.

"I suppose," Stacey finally said, "that Nancy came upon her when she got up. Nancy alerted me to the tragedy before she left."

"So Nancy came to you before she went away. She left me sleeping and came to you."

"She came to say goodbye."

"To your room."

Stacey stopped moving down the stairs, causing Steve to bump into him and nearly drop his end of the dog. "Yes, to my room," said Stacey.

"She saw your room?"

Stacey resumed moving, and after a brief hesitation, Steve followed. "I guess so," said Stacey. "From the doorway."

"She didn't come in?"

"Of course not. That would have been inappropriate. She's

married to you, not me. A lady should not come into the bed chambers of a man who's not her husband."

"What did she say?"

"I don't remember her exact words. Maybe, 'Stacey, your dog isn't well. I think she's sick. Maybe dead. I'm heading out now.'"

"And she left then? Just like that?"

"Just like that."

"She didn't follow you back into the room?"

"No."

"What about the typed note?"

They finally reached the bottom of the stairs, where Stacey stopped to catch his breath, clearly winded from the exertion of navigating the steps and talking at the same time. He clutched his chest as sweat flowed from every pore of his body.

"I'm trying to understand when she typed the note," said Steve. He and Leslie still held the dog as they waited for Stacey to compose himself.

"Before she left," Stacey said, still holding his chest, each word loaded with exasperation. "I don't know. I needed to call Leslie. I hoped he would help. I didn't want to wake you."

He studied Steve's expression as his breathing began to steady.

"Is that satisfactory? That I would call my friend to come help me with my *dead fucking dog?*"

Steve nodded. They finished their labor in silence, with Stacey directing the other two outside, where he instructed them to load the carcass into the bed of his truck. As they completed the task, Steve's eyes scanned the area.

"I'm telling the truth," Stacey said. "She's gone."

Steve said nothing. What could he say? His car was gone.

"Since you won't be going anywhere for a while," Stacey said,

"I have another favor to ask you."

16

"Get Your Shovel, Old Man"

The three of them rode in silence. Like before, Stacey did the driving, but this time, Steve sat where Nancy did previously—in the rear with the broken seat belt. Leslie's size necessitated him taking the front seat next to Stacey, whose driving seemed markedly different from before. No swerving or speeding up. None of the constant, violent braking that earlier threw around his passengers with bruising force. He stopped for traffic lights. He obeyed speed limits. He used his turn signal. He hit no curbs. He drove perfectly.

At one point, Stacey finally broke the silence by saying, "I'm taking extra care for Leslie. When he was a professional wrestler, he developed a chronic ear problem. It causes him to get car sick very easily."

Steve didn't reply. He stared at the object he held in the palm of his hand.

Stacey went on: "The accident in the ring? The one that killed his opponent? It wasn't Leslie's fault. His opponent simply wasn't conditioned enough."

Leslie nodded but apparently had nothing to add.

"What's in your hand, Steven?" asked Stacey.

Steve closed his fist around the tiny cross. "It's nothing," he said, tucking it into his pocket.

"I'll see if my mother lost an earring," said Stacey.

"It's not an earring. But okay, you do that."

The sun rose sluggishly, unable the penetrate the lingering clouds. Everything around them looked tired and angry, but at least the water had begun to recede, and nothing impeded their journey.

"Is this the—"

"Yes," Stacey said before Steve could finish.

The truck slowed and came to a stop before the hanging tree that Stacey showed Steve and Nancy on their tour. The light seemed even dimmer here, thanks to the spread of the tree's expansive limbs.

Stacey put the truck in park and began the process of extracting himself from the driver's seat. Leslie moved much faster, positioning himself outside Steve's door.

Steve made no attempt to get out. "Why are we here?"

"I'm going to show you how we do things," Stacey said. His breathing sounded heavy as usual, only not from exertion this time. More from excitement.

Steve leaned forward so he could see the tree through the truck's windshield.

Finally, Leslie opened Steve's door and offered him his hand. His eyes looked like those of a shark waiting for the aquarium glass to break.

"I don't understand what this is about." Steve spoke to the large hand extended to him as if it might speak back.

Outside the truck, Stacey moved purposely to Steve's side of the vehicle. A night of sleep had done wonders for his knees.

He practically glided. "You saw my big bag of lime before, didn't you? I noticed how you looked at it."

Steve's lips moved, but no words came out.

"Would you please accept Leslie's assistance and get out of the truck? We really shouldn't be here when the light finally comes up."

When Steve didn't move, Leslie reached forth and took him by the wrist. For such a large man, his touch proved surprisingly gentle. Steve didn't resist, and soon, all three stood outside the truck.

"Good," Stacey said. "Now, you and Leslie take Scratchy, and I'll get the bag of lime."

Once more, Steve and Leslie each took an end of the blanket wrapped around the dog's remains. Walking sideways, they began moving toward the tree. Stacey walked behind them, the bag of lime slung over his right shoulder. He only needed one arm to keep it in place.

"Where are we going?" Steve asked after nearly stumbling on a tree root.

"Isn't it obvious? Over there." Stacey used his free hand to point toward the ancient Gullah cemetery. "Not much farther."

The purple light became pink as they came upon the graves. At one point, Steve's foot sank into wet soil, delaying their progress. They all stopped and watched as Steve tried to pull himself free. When he finally did, his foot came away with just a sock, the shoe now sunk beneath the earth. Steve proceeded without protest, leaving the shoe behind.

"Someone's going to have to remember to get that shoe later." These words came with a syrupy drawl, one familiar to Steve.

Even though it sounded nothing like Nancy's voice, his head still snapped hopefully in its direction. "Nancy?" he said. In the process, he dropped his end of the blanket, eliciting an irritated noise from Leslie.

But the voice belonged to Pepper, the woman he met at the thrift store. Wearing a tank top damp with sweat, she leaned against a shovel and nearly blended into the surroundings. Not far from her, Jaspar, the antiquarian in charge of the "museum," sat on something low to ground, a pick-ax on the ground near his feet. Across from them, the apparent results of their labor— an open hole with a mound of earth laying off to the side.

"Everything's under control, Pepper," Stacey said. "Steven, would you please pick up your end so that Leslie doesn't have to carry that thing by himself?"

"We had to do this by ourselves," said Jaspar, still seated on an object hard to discern in the gloomy half-light.

Pepper nodded. "And I don't know what your idea of 'under control' is if I got to come pick up after you." She reached into her shorts and pulled out the "receipt" she gave to Steve earlier. She waved it toward Steve. "I thought you were going to come back. I thought for sure you were. You sure did hurt my feelings by throwing it away."

"Waste of time. The rain would've turned it pulp," Jaspar said.

"Says you. They got machines that can read the writing on the toilet paper you used to wipe your ass."

Stacey ignored them as he walked further and dropped the bag of lime close to the edge of the empty grave.

"Thought for sure you'd come back," Pepper said again. Then she laughed hideously. Jaspar joined in.

Steve stood motionless and studied the faces in the group. Each one regarded him back.

"I want to know what we're doing here," he said when they stopped laughing.

"I don't like doing this when the sun's up," Pepper said. She spit something on the ground.

"We're doing something perfectly natural," said Stacey. "Did you get a good look at the skeletons in the Jungle Room, Steven? This is how I do it. You and Leslie need to drop poor Scratchy into this hole, and then we cover him with lime. Then we'll wait a reasonable amount of time and come back to dig him up. When we do, we'll find just a skeleton. The lime speeds up the process. It's natural and beautiful. This way, Scratchy lives forever. Just like every Scratchy before her."

Everyone became quiet and waited for Steve to say something.

Finally, he spoke. "Why here? That seems disrespectful to me."

"No one minds," Stacey said. "It's public land, and it's one of the highest elevations on the whole island. If you look in that direction, you might be able to see water."

Steve squinted in the direction Stacey pointed.

"It's fine, Steven. Nothing to worry about. Please help out."

"Yeah, 'cause I ain't doing it," said Jaspar. "Already broke my back by digging." He shook his head. "No white man should endure what I went through."

A moment of hesitation as Steve once more studied their faces. Finally, he picked up his end of the blanket, and together, he and Leslie carried it to the empty grave. There, Steve let his end fall, resulting in another frustrated grunt from the former wrestler, who, by contrast, set his side down gently and carefully. Then he rolled the dog's carcass into the hole, where it landed with a thump.

"There," Stacey said. "Was that so difficult?"

"You got enough in that bag?" asked Pepper.

"Enough for what?" Steve asked. He stretched his back and swiveled his hips.

"Oh, god," Stacey said, "I forgot all about your back injury. Are you in pain?"

"Listen to that," said Jaspar. "We're out here digging two holes, and I don't hear him asking about our backs."

At the mention of *two* holes, Steve's eyes scanned the area until they came to the second one, not ten feet away.

"What's that one for?" he asked.

Pepper and Jaspar chuckled.

"You're right, old man, that was hard work," Pepper said. "You got something cold to drink in there?"

Jaspar looked under his rump, his expression feigning surprise. "I forgot all about that."

Without his ass in the way, everyone could see the thing under him—a large blue and white cooler. The one that Steve and Nancy kept in their back seat during their travels.

"Nope," Jaspar said as he gazed into the open cooler, "ain't nothing to drink in here."

"That's shitty planning," Pepper said.

"Wasn't no room." He closed the cooler and resumed his seat. Staring at Steve, he repeated it. "Wasn't no room."

"Plenty of room now," Pepper said.

"Sticky, though. I wouldn't drink anything that comes out of there."

Steve and Jaspar continued staring at each other, neither blinking.

"I know what you're thinking, Steven," said Stacey. "You see us digging here, and you think it's grave robbing. Well, I wouldn't call it that. Most of the time, there isn't anyone under these markers. They're just there to fool people. To trick us.

We find other things beneath the dirt." He whispered the next word. *"Treasure."*

Steve said nothing, the staring contest unbroken.

"Go and look if you don't believe me," said Stacey. "That one has quite a treasure in it." He pointed toward the second open grave.

Leslie and Stacey followed Steve toward the edge of the hole. From Pepper and Jaspar came muffled laughter. A breeze scattered droplets of rain from the trees overhead.

Steve stopped and turned to Stacey before he reached the pit. "Why are they worried about having enough lime?" Tears began streaming down his face.

"It's expensive. I like to save it. Why are you crying, Steven?"

"I'm not crying." But Steve wiped his face.

"Is it because of what happened to Carla all those years ago?"

Steve didn't answer. He resumed walking until his feet reached the edge of the hole. He would not look in it.

"Maybe you're crying because your back hurts so much." Stacey paused as Leslie whispered something in his ear. He nodded and then said, "If you want, Leslie can fix your back again."

Steve regarded Stacey as his eyes continued to cloud with tears. He avoided looking down.

Leslie whispered something else to Stacey and then advanced closer to Steve, standing right behind him now. Still holding her shovel, Pepper walked closer. Grumbling, Jaspar hoisted himself off the cooler and followed her.

"Leslie likes tips," said Stacey. "Before he fixes your back again, do you mind tipping him?"

For a moment, Steve looked like he would bolt, and Pepper moved even closer, both hands on the shovel. Instead, Steve reached into his pocket and drew forth the small cross. He held it out for Leslie to take. Leslie stared at the object in his big hand and chuckled softly. Then he tucked into his pocket. With a gentle hand, he turned Steve so that he faced away from him and toward the hole.

Stacey said, "Do you really not remember what happened with Carla?"

"I don't know. Everything is so mixed up in my head. I can't think."

"I know it's hard, Steven. To help you, I want you to look down. Not at the ground. Into the hole."

Steve hesitated. Everyone could see he didn't want to look. Finally, Leslie took his head in his giant hands and tilted Steve's head for him.

"Open your eyes, Steven."

At first, it looked as if Steve would refuse and that Leslie might to do it for him. But finally, Steve looked. His mouth tensed into a grimace, the face of a man about to become sick.

"I know it's hard to look at. But you know what? I'm taking responsibility for what you're seeing down there. I didn't even do it. I found her like that. Dead. But I'm man enough to stand before you now and say that I'm sorry. In the future, I'll keep things more secure. If it helps to know, I bowed my head and said a little prayer after we put her into the cooler. She looked very peaceful."

Steve pressed his fist to his mouth and cried.

"So I've taken responsibility. Are you ready to take responsibility too, Steven? For what happened to Carla?"

"I am." Steve's breath hitched as a sob escaped his lips. "I'm sorry for that. For everything." Tears ran down his face freely. He didn't try to hide his sobbing. "Please forgive me." He looked at all their faces. He even turned to Leslie. "All of you, please forgive me. Let me go."

"Shit, I think I'm going to cry too, and I didn't even have a beef with this motherfucker," said Jaspar.

Stacey cried as well. "It's okay, Steven. I forgive you now."

Steve tried to walk away. Maybe to escape. Maybe to go to Stacey and wrap his arms around him. But Leslie chose that moment to grab him. This time, he wrapped all ten of his fingers around Steve's neck and lifted him from his feet. The others watched as the former wrestler held Steve above the ground as his body twisted and his legs kicked at nothing but air, thanks to the strength of Leslie's trunk-like arms. They all stood motionless, marveling at Leslie's impressive ability to hold a full-grown man off the ground as he used his hands to crush his throat, squeezing so hard that they could hear the bones in his neck cracking and breaking. Then came the sound of gurgling, air struggling through a broken and twisted windpipe. The whole time, Leslie maintained the same stance, his feet steady and arms unwavering, all his training and athleticism developed for this one moment—to end Steve's life.

It took several minutes for all movement in Steve's body to cease, all function to end.

Then Leslie dropped him into the hole on top of Nancy's body.

Stacey took a deep breath before putting on a pair of rubber gloves and emptying the rest of the lime on top of the remains. Then he stared down into the hole. From the tree behind them came the sound of birds, their song celebrating a new day free of rain.

"Get your shovel, old man," said Pepper. "Time to work."

"Not enough lime for two of them," said her cohort. "I want

clean bones. Waste of effort." But he picked up his shovel anyway.

As the two of them began shoveling dirt, the man looked at Stacey. "We won't turn down help, you know."

Leslie spoke up now. In a soft, tender voice, he said to Jaspar, "Leave him be. He's lost his cousin. This has been hard for him. Time has been hard for him."

Then Leslie put his arms around Stacey, the only arms in the world big enough to encompass his friend's body, and he held him close and squeezed gently, whispering consoling words that no one else could hear. Stacey accepted the embrace, allowing his friend to soothe him as the sun finished rising and the birds rejoiced.

Acknowledgments

While I never want to experience a road trip like the one that Steve and Nancy take, I do love to travel, and I'm lucky enough to be married to someone who enjoys an adventure. Jerlin Ford not only knows how to plan a vacation, but she makes every day an adventure. She also provided a terrific sounding board as I drafted this book.

My parents, Herb and Sally, took me on many road trips when they raised me. My love of travel begins with them. They also encouraged me to write and exercise my creativity. There would be no books without them.

I'm very grateful to Lisa Lee Tone for her editing. She is simply the best in the business. Speaking of the best, the cover art comes from Don Noble, who creates some of the most dazzling images in the horror business.

To Kenzie Jennings and Ruth Anna Evans, thank you for reading an early version of the book's manuscript and offering your thoughts and praise. Also, a shout-out to my good friends, Holly Rae Garcia, Matthew Masucci, and Elaine Pascale—thank you both for the moral support!

Finally, thank you to you, whoever you are, for reading this book. Always count the traffic lights and place cautious trust in your G.P.S.

About the Author

Douglas Ford writes horror fiction while also chairing the Southwest Florida chapter of the Horror Writers Association. He has written two other collections of short fiction, APE IN THE RING & OTHER TALES OF THE MACABRE AND UNCANNY and THE INFECTION PARTY AND OTHER STORIES OF DIS-EASE. His novels and novellas include THE TRICK, THE BEASTS OF VISSARIA COUNTY, THE LAST SLAUGHTER, THE REATTACHMENT, and the award-winning LITTLE LUGOSI (A LOVE STORY).

You can connect with me on:

🌐 https://douglasfordwrites.com

f https://www.facebook.com/profile.php?id=100064149938106